She had to stand her ground.

There was no other choice. "If we're going to be working together, don't you think we should clear the air?"

Clay made a soft sound in his throat. "Clearing the air won't change anything. Besides, who says we'll be working together?"

Her heart sank. She took a second to level off her emotions. Clay had been easygoing, fun and very romantic. It was why she'd fallen in love with him so quickly. Love at first sight for both of them. "I don't remember you being so coldhearted."

"Really? Well, do you remember me asking you to marry me?"

Her knees nearly buckled. She didn't want to go down this path. "Yes, but…"

"Do you remember saying it was a big decision and you needed time to think things over? Do you remember stealing away like a thief in the night without a word of explanation or even a goodbye?"

Her heart was being shredded but she refused to cry in front of him. She nodded and breathed a soft yes.

Lorraine Beatty was raised in Columbus, Ohio, but now calls Mississippi home. She and her husband, Joe, have two sons and five grandchildren. Lorraine started writing in junior high and is a member of RWA and ACFW, and is a charter member and past president of Magnolia State Romance Writers. In her spare time she likes to work in her garden, travel and spend time with her family.

Books by Lorraine Beatty

Love Inspired

The Orphans' Blessing
Her Secret Hope

Mississippi Hearts

Her Fresh Start Family
Their Family Legacy
Their Family Blessing

Home to Dover

Protecting the Widow's Heart
His Small-Town Family
Bachelor to the Rescue
Her Christmas Hero
The Nanny's Secret Child
A Mom for Christmas
The Lawman's Secret Son
Her Handyman Hero

Visit the Author Profile page
at Harlequin.com for more titles.

Her Secret Hope

Lorraine Beatty

LOVE INSPIRED
INSPIRATIONAL ROMANCE

LOVE INSPIRED®
INSPIRATIONAL ROMANCE

Recycling programs
for this product may
not exist in your area.

ISBN-13: 978-1-335-48881-7

Her Secret Hope

Copyright © 2021 by Lorraine Beatty

This edition published by arrangement with Harlequin Books S.A.

For questions and comments about the quality of this book,
please contact us at CustomerService@Harlequin.com.

Love Inspired
22 Adelaide St. West, 40th Floor
Toronto, Ontario M5H 4E3, Canada
www.Harlequin.com

Printed in U.S.A.

Hath not the potter power over the clay, of the same lump to make one vessel unto honour, and another unto dishonour?
—*Romans* 9:21

Dedicated to my sweet husband, Joe.
My friend, my love, my ideal man.

Chapter One

Melody Williams stopped to admire the two-story limestone building at the corner of Blessing, Mississippi's downtown square. The courthouse annex was a 1920s art deco treasure. Its wide welcoming steps and ornate arch above the door beckoned visitors to come and explore. Like everything else in the small Southern town, it oozed charm. Much of her anxiety over taking the job with the Blessing Bicentennial Commission eased. Reporting to work in this historic structure each day to write and photograph the town's history would be the best decision she'd made in a long time.

Pulling open the heavy wood-and-glass door, she stopped at the reception desk for directions to Councilman Reynolds's office. Her anxiety stirred as she knocked on his door. She tugged on her shirtsleeve. She couldn't fail at this job. It was her last chance to find her way back to wholeness and follow the path the Lord had laid out for her. Unless she'd gotten it all wrong. Again.

Her dream of being an international correspondent had ended when terrorists bombed the Shanghai office where she worked, leaving her fighting for her life and mourning the loss of most of her coworkers.

"Come in."

A slender, gray-haired man with twinkling blue eyes and a generous smile met her with his hand outstretched. "Ah, Miss Williams. Welcome to Blessing. I can't tell you how excited we all are for you to write our history. The whole town is ready to help out in any way possible."

He perched on the edge of his desk and gestured to a nearby chair, still grinning. "You're much younger than I expected. I think we were assuming you'd be a mature librarian type."

She smiled. "I'm like that on the inside."

Reynolds laughed. "Good one. You're going to fit in well here."

"I'm glad. I look forward to working with you, Mr. Reynolds." She'd imagined all kinds of city councilman types on her drive down here from Iowa, everything from the puffed-up, self-important men, to the sour, unibrowed, grouchy types. The warm-and-friendly Mr. Reynolds was a delightful surprise.

He grinned and moved behind his desk. "Call me Dave. However, you'll mainly be working with my son. He's the chairman of the book project."

"Oh. I assumed you were in charge of the bicentennial."

"No, only part of it. The Blessing Merchants Guild shares the responsibility." He poked a button on his phone. "Hey, champ. Can you stop by my office? The book lady is here."

Melody smothered a smile. *Book lady* did make her sound like an old maid, but then again, at thirty-two years old, she felt like one most of the time.

"He'll be right here. He knows a lot about Blessing. Our family goes back four generations in this town."

Melody tried not to anticipate what was to come, but if the son was as charming as his dad, she would enjoy this assignment very much. She heard the door open behind her, then soft footsteps on the carpet.

"Son, this is M. J. Williams. Our book lady."

She turned her head and extended her hand. Her gaze landed on a tall, dark-haired man with gorgeous eyes and a cleft chin just like—her heart stopped beating. Burning heat and icy chills chased through her body. Blood surged in her ears, and her cheeks flamed. All the while, her mind screamed *no!*

From the look on the man's face, he wasn't thrilled to see her either. His jaw locked and his eyes narrowed. She couldn't help but notice how the blue in his plaid shirt rivaled the vibrant color of those eyes. He took her hand but released it quickly as if afraid of being burned. She looked away, waiting for the world to come crashing down.

"Miss Williams, my son, Clay." Mr. Reynolds frowned. "Are you all right? You look flushed."

Melody struggled to speak through the dryness in her mouth. "Just a little case of nerves." She braced for Clay to blow the lid off her life. He'd tell his dad who she was, that she'd walked out on him without a word and never looked back. Instead, he remained silent, though rigid and vibrating with emotion.

"I think you're going to like this young lady, son. She's a good one."

A stiff smile barely moved Clay's lips. "I'm sure."

"Okay. I have some information to get you started, Miss Williams. It's an overview of Blessing." Dave handed her a thick folder with a picture of a bridge on the cover. "I'll have Clay show you to your office. I'm sure you'll want to get settled first. You can report for work in a day or so."

"Oh, that's kind of you but I'd like to get started as soon as possible." Unless Clay sent her packing—which looked like a good possibility at the moment.

"Wonderful. I like your enthusiasm." He pointed to Clay. "I told you she was the right one. As a matter of fact, why don't you give Miss Melody a tour of our fair city. Help her get her bearings."

"Of course."

Melody held her tight smile until she and Clay were in the hallway. She stole a glance, but he was walking briskly, eyes forward, the muscle in his jaw twitching like a live electrical wire. Her gaze followed the length of his form, from his muscled back to the dark jeans that hugged his long legs. She had to step quickly to keep up.

The silence between them grew painful. "Clay."

He stopped and opened a door at the end of the hall. "It's not much, but it's the only space we had."

She stepped inside the tiny room. "This will be fine. I don't plan to spend much time here anyway. I'll be out doing research and conducting interviews." Of course, that all depended on whether she still had a job.

"What are you doing here?"

She winced at the harsh tone in his voice and answered without looking at him. "I'm the book lady. What are you doing here?"

"I live here. Or have you forgotten?"

She searched her brain for a memory of him telling her where he lived, but came up empty. "I didn't know... Or I didn't remember."

He snorted. "I'd guess there's a lot you don't remember. But you shouldn't be here."

The accusation in his tone stung. "Clay. If you want me to leave, I can't do that. I need this job."

A sardonic smile lifted one corner of his mouth. "The big international news correspondent gig didn't work out?"

His barb hit true. If only he knew. She prayed for courage, then faced him. "Life has a way of changing things."

"Yeah. I know."

She raised her chin. She had to stand her ground. There was no other choice. "If we're going to be working together, we should probably clear the air."

Clay made a soft sound in his throat. "Clearing the air won't change anything. Besides, who says we'll be working together?"

Her heart sank. She took a second to level off her emotions. Clay had been easygoing, fun and very romantic. It's why she'd fallen in love with him so quickly. Love at first sight for both. "I don't remember you being coldhearted."

"Really? Well, do you remember me asking you to marry me?"

Her knees nearly buckled. "Yes, but—"

"Do you remember saying it was a big decision and you needed time to think things over? Do you remember stealing away without a word of explanation or even a goodbye?"

Every word clawed at her heart, but she would not cry in front of him. He had no concept of what she'd gone through or what she'd given up. She nodded and breathed a soft yes.

"Huh. Seems your memory isn't completely gone, then. I don't think we have anything else to say, do you?" Clay squared his shoulders. "Unless you had your heart set on that tour of Blessing."

She shook her head. "I can find my own way around."

But he'd already pivoted and walked off.

Melody dropped her papers on the desk and sank into the nearest chair. How was he here? Of all the people in the world she had never expected—never *wanted*—to see again, Clay Reynolds was the one. She'd stuffed that part of her life deep inside and buried it under layers of guilt and denial. *Lord, I can't do this.*

Tears threatened behind her eyes. If Clay fired her, she didn't know what she would do next. She was so weary from the last two years recuperating and fighting her way back to some semblance of a normal life.

Picking up the folder Dave had given her, she slipped out the exit door at the end of the hall and hurried to her car. She needed to think. No, she needed to talk to Sandy. She'd understand.

She and her foster sister had always been on the same wavelength. Sandy's friendship and encouragement were why she was here in the first place. If this job with the bicentennial committee fell through, she was out of hope.

Clay's jaw had started to ache from clenching his teeth. How had he not realized that Melody was the one they'd hired to compile the Blessing history book? He never would have agreed to it if he'd known. Ever. He'd spent the last ten years trying to forget she existed.

He marched into his dad's office, his emotions roiling like a hurricane. "We can't use her."

"Who?"

"Williams. She's all wrong for the job."

"What are you talking about? You're the one who

chose her." He frowned and leaned back in his chair. "What's going on?"

Clay exhaled slowly. He had chosen her, but he hadn't realized she was *Melody*, the woman who'd stolen his heart at first sight. The woman he'd fallen head over heels in love with. They'd spent every moment together, one fateful summer. He'd never felt so connected to anyone before. She was his missing piece…until she'd shredded his heart and soul and left him bleeding.

"I can't work with her."

"Why not? She seems like a charming young woman who's excited to start on the book." He peered over the rim of his reading glasses. "Care to explain what's going on?"

Clay rubbed his chin. How much should he admit to? He'd never told his father the whole truth about what had happened back then. At the time, he'd thought it best for everyone concerned to keep certain things secret. He still did. Coming clean now wouldn't be good for his father's health. Since that minor stroke last year, Clay had done everything in his power to keep his dad's life as free of stress as possible. Telling him about Melody now could be dangerous.

Clay's cell played the iconic notes from *SportsCenter*. He welcomed the interruption. "Hey, Eli." He listened as his son asked permission to go to Jacob's house to play video games. "Fine, but I'll be by around three to pick you up. I have a spray this afternoon."

Dave Reynolds removed his glasses and smiled. "What's that grandson of mine up to now?"

Clay slipped the phone in his pocket. "Video games with a friend."

Dad shook his head. "I hope you're monitoring his

time on that stuff. I don't want him living in your basement when he's thirty."

"We don't have basements here."

Dave waved off his comment. "Well, you know what I'm saying."

"Yeah, I know." His father adored his grandson almost as much as Clay did. Eli was the light of his life, his reason for getting up each day and the reason he'd fought so hard to protect him. And he would go on doing that as long as he drew breath.

"So, about Miss Williams. We need to clear this up. What has you all fired up about her anyway?"

"I didn't know she was the one you hired, that's all."

"Of course you did. You read her résumé, and we agreed on her qualifications." He reached over and picked up a paper from his desk. "I have it right here. There's her name at the bottom."

Clay took the paper, staring at the bottom line. M. J. Williams. His heart sank. He remembered glancing over the applications, but he hadn't paid much attention because it didn't seem important. It was only a history book after all. "I didn't know it was Melody."

"Do you know this woman? Why didn't you say so?"

"No. I just—" How did he explain? He'd avoided the subject for ten years. He'd told his dad the truth about Eli, but not all of it.

"If you can't give me a good reason for letting her go, then she stays. We have a deadline for this book if it's going to be published in time for the bicentennial next year. There's no time to find someone else who's as qualified as she is."

He was trapped. An explanation would only make things worse for everyone. "You're right."

"So you'll work with her?"

"Sure, Dad."

"Good. Did I hear you say you had a spray this afternoon?"

"The Clawson farm."

"Good. I don't know what our business would do without them. They're our biggest customer. Be careful up there."

Clay mulled over his father's words as he drove back to the family home a few miles out of town, his gaze catching on the sign at the entrance to their drive. Dusty Birds Aerial Application. Three generations of Reynolds men were crop dusters, and their company was the largest in the tricounty area. He only hoped it would remain that way. Competition from a new company in northern Mississippi, Delta Agricultural Applications, was growing, and Clay had already lost two customers to them. It hadn't impacted their business significantly yet, so he hadn't burdened his dad with that worry right now.

Clay drove past the sprawling family home to the small hangar and private airstrip behind. He was looking forward to being in the air. He'd be too busy to think about Melody turning up in Blessing and threatening his world.

He parked and started across the field to the yellow Air Tractor he'd be flying today. What would his father say if he told him that Melody was Eli's mother? That she'd given him up for adoption? Clay had told everyone she had died when Eli was born. How could he come clean now?

He bowed his head and closed his eyes. How did he keep up his facade with her in town? He had so much to lose. He had to keep the truth to himself. It was the only way.

* * *

Melody stopped at the intersection, her blinker signaling a right turn toward Sandy's house. As she waited for an oncoming car to pass, her gaze landed on the folder beside her, the one with the bridge on the cover. Sandy had told her about the Blessing Bridge soon after she'd arrived. It was one of the first places she'd planned to research for the book. Well, now was the perfect time to get started. She was in desperate need of spiritual guidance.

Switching off her blinker, she drove on Main Street until she saw the historic marker for the bridge. Pulling into the small parking lot, she took a moment to flip open the folder and read the brief history of the landmark.

"In the mid-1950s, a woman whose son had polio came to the bridge and prayed for healing. Three weeks later, her son started to improve. Three weeks after that, he was cured. People started coming to the bridge and reporting amazing answers to their prayers."

Melody didn't need answers so much as comfort and strength. She had to succeed at this job. If she failed, there was nothing else open to her. Her journalism career was over. Her hopes of a professional photography career lacked the credentials to land a job that would support her. If she could do a good job with this history, it would prove she could move forward again. That she had value as a journalist in the future.

Her mind traveled back in time to the worst choice she'd ever made. She'd been bursting with ambition and on a path that would give her the sense of worth she'd always craved. She couldn't help but wonder how her life would have evolved if she'd chosen the better way. The less selfish way.

Melody started toward the path leading into the thick woods. She stopped and read the plaque beside the entrance. *The Blessing Bridge. A place of hope and peace. Lift your cares to the Lord with a sincere heart and a humble spirit and return renewed.*

The path was clogged with underbrush and uneven in spots. She would have expected it to be more user-friendly. Finally, it emerged into sunlight and revealed the former gardens. Despite the overgrown state, the surroundings were lovely and hinted at the beauty that had once graced the area. The bridge, an old wooden structure with peeling white paint, arched gracefully over a large pond choked with water plants and algae.

Stopping at the crest of the bridge, she scanned the landscape, taking a few pictures with her phone. She'd bring her camera next time. It would capture the peace and solitude of the landmark better than her cell could ever do.

At the moment, she needed to focus on her own spiritual state. She closed her eyes briefly and offered up gratitude for the opportunity she'd been given. Then she opened her eyes and let her vision take in the view. Even with its neglected condition, there was a serene peace about the bridge. She could see why people flocked here to offer up their prayers. Hers was a simple one today. She asked for strength to withstand Clay's reappearance in her life, and the ability to do her best on creating the Blessing history book.

The Lord had provided for her every step of the way since the bombing in Shanghai, and she knew He would see her through this assignment, too. She just needed to keep her focus. Her gaze traveled to the distant trees, and her attention fell on the ruins of an old plantation

home. She leaned over the bridge railing for a closer
look. The house had no roof, and the large columns on
the front were wrapped in dead gray vines that lent an
eerie quality to the remnants of the once-proud man-
sion. Her curiosity was engaged. She would have to
learn more about the historic dwelling, and then she'd
come back for pictures. There might be enough here
alone to fill a chapter in the book.

She started back to her car. Normally she felt renewed after time in prayer, but today she felt drained
and tired. It was time to talk to her sister.

Sandy Hackett was sitting on her front porch when
Melody pulled her car into the drive and climbed out.
She'd barely made the top step before Sandy demanded
to know what was wrong.

"Uh-oh. What happened? Did you get fired already?"

"Probably."

"What? I was joking. What happened?"

"Clay happened?"

Sandy pulled her down beside her on the porch swing.
"Clay? What's he have to do with anything? He's a great
guy. Blessing's most eligible single dad."

Melody stared at her friend. "Clay's a dad?"

"Uh-huh. He has a little boy. Eli. Great kid."

Clay. A dad. It made sense. He'd always been a family-
and-forever kind of guy. That's why she'd walked away.
She knew little about being part of a family. "I didn't
know he was married."

"She died when Eli was a baby. He doesn't talk about
it. Too painful. So what do you have against him?"

Melody's mind whirled. She should keep the truth
to herself, but she needed someone to understand, and

Sandy was the only person in the world she could trust. "Clay is the man I was in love with when—"

Sandy gasped. "You mean he's the father of the baby you gave up? Oh, Melly. I'm so sorry. Of all the places to end up. I wish I hadn't told you about this job. I had no idea. What are you going to do?"

"I don't know. He was furious when he saw me. He wants me off the project. But you know how much I need this job." She tugged at her shirtsleeve. "Working is the only thing that keeps me sane."

Sandy took her hand. "Is Clay the reason you never loved anyone else?"

"No!" Except she knew the moment she said the word that it was a lie. No one had ever made her feel the way Clay had. Happy. Content. Like she'd finally belonged to someone.

"Maybe. I guess."

"Then this is your chance to take a different path. You and Clay can mend the past and start fresh."

"No. Our relationship is broken. It can't be mended."

Sandy pointed a finger at her. "Jesus came for the broken, remember?"

She wanted to draw comfort from her sister's sincere reminder, but having seen Clay again, it was clear that he would never forgive her, and she couldn't blame him. She would never forgive herself.

Supper with Sandy's family was a lively event and Melody tried to enjoy it, but she was relieved when they all settled down for the night. It had been a stressful day, and she longed for sleep. But first, she wanted to look over the folder Dave had given her. It would give her a starting point on the book.

A few minutes later, she gave up and turned out

the light. Her brain was too tired to work tonight. She tugged the covers up to her chin, resisting the urge to cover her head. She was grateful to Sandy for offering her space in her home, but sleeping on a hide-a-bed in the living room made a restful night impossible. Finding a quiet place of her own was at the top of her to-do list.

Determined not to worry about what tomorrow would bring, Melody settled down and willed herself to sleep. The moment her eyes were closed, however, a vision of Clay filled her head. The years had been kind to him. He'd grown from a slender young man into a stronger, more solid version of himself. His shoulders displayed the breadth of a full-grown man. His hair was a darker shade of brown now, more black coffee than a warm earth tone. The tiny lines around his eyes and mouth added character and strength. He'd grown even more handsome than she'd remembered. She drifted off with visions of Clay swirling in her mind.

The explosion brought her bolt upright in bed. Her heart pounded. Sweat ran down her spine. She sucked air into her lungs. Her vision cleared. Her heart rate began to slow.

She was in Sandy's living room, not an office in Shanghai. She waited for some sign that she'd wakened the family, but the house was still. Drawing up her knees, she scraped her fingers through her hair, then lowered her head. It had been months since she'd had a nightmare. She'd started to believe they were gone, though her therapist had warned her they could still be triggered by stress. Like running into her child's father after ten years.

Lying back down, she stared at the ceiling. She wouldn't be sleeping anymore tonight. It would make for a long, difficult day tomorrow.

Chapter Two

Clay was still replaying the moment yesterday when he'd seen Melody sitting in his dad's office. Her presence in Blessing had kept him restless all night. Seeing her again had unleashed a torrent of anger, humiliation and betrayal. The memory of her walking out on him ten years ago still had the power to rake over him like a sharpened pitchfork.

He'd loved her. Passionately, deeply and in a way he'd never experienced before. They'd known each other only a short while, but he'd wanted it to go on forever, which is why he'd had the ring in his pocket that day. He'd been so sure she'd felt the same way, until she'd told him she was pregnant. His emotions had knotted into a snarled mess of happiness, shock and remorse. He'd asked her to marry him, but she'd hesitated, mumbling something about needing time to think, and her career. She'd promised to give him an answer in the morning, but the next morning she was gone. No note. No phone call. No way to get in touch.

Clay shoved the past back into the recesses of his

mind. Reliving the end of their relationship served no purpose.

He headed downstairs and into the kitchen, where the tantalizing aromas of breakfast drew a rumble from his stomach. He smiled and laid a hand on his father's shoulder. "It smells great, Dad." He hated to think what his life would be like without his father... But it was time to tell him the truth. He just had to find the right moment. And the right words.

"How did your tour with Melody go yesterday? Was she impressed with our little town?"

Clay took the plate of eggs, hash browns and bacon and sat at the round breakfast table. "I didn't give her the tour. She wanted to find her own way around. She's a very independent woman."

His dad poured a cup of coffee and placed it in front of Clay. "I wanted you two to go together. You need to establish a good relationship. I want this history to be comprehensive, and it won't be if you two are at loggerheads. She needs your input."

"I know, Dad. I'll find a way to make it work."

Dave sat down. "I don't understand. What can you possibly have against Melody? She's pretty, smart and supremely qualified. Not to mention delightful."

Clay cradled his mug in his hands. The longer he postponed this the worse it would be. "Dad. Melody Williams is Eli's mother."

Footsteps on the hallway floor announced Eli's arrival. Clay was thankful his son hadn't overheard his revelation. Eli entered the kitchen. "Oh, good. Grandpa fixed breakfast. I love it when he cooks."

Dave stood and helped Eli prepare a plate. The boy attacked it with the gusto only a ten-year-old could produce, gulping his juice between bites. "Dad, can we have a flying lesson today?"

Clay marveled at the simplicity of youth. Eli's world consisted of school, ball teams, video games and learning to fly. "I'll see if we can squeeze one in. I have a long list of fields to treat today."

"Awesome."

"You'd better go brush your teeth or you'll miss the bus." Clay watched his son climb onto the yellow bus a few minutes later, then returned to the kitchen.

Dad was still sitting at the table, his shoulders hunched. Waiting. He couldn't postpone this any longer. Clay poured another cup of coffee, then joined his dad. Dave set down his mug, then clasped his hands together. A sure indication of his distress.

"You told me Eli's mother had died."

A rush of heat lanced through Clay. "I know, Dad. It just seemed easier at the time."

"Easier to lie to your father? To everyone?" He pressed his lips together; his blue eyes, like lasers, pinned Clay to the chair. "You know, I've always had a bad feeling about this. That year you were in Atlanta, the lack of contact. Of course, you claimed you were studying for your master's."

"I was. I did… But there were other things going on, as well."

"Obviously." Dave shook his head. "I should have paid closer attention, but your mother had just been diagnosed and I wasn't thinking of much else. I should have paid more attention to your situation." A look of horror appeared on his face. "Please tell me Eli is really your son."

"Yes. He is. I wouldn't lie about that."

"But you would about everything else?"

Clay faced his father. "I'm not proud of that part of my life. It was a mistake. I was getting ready to ask her to marry me when she told me she was pregnant. And I did, but she said she had to think about it. Then she disappeared—left without another word. I tracked her down and learned she was planning on giving the baby away. My child. I couldn't let that happen, so I arranged to adopt him myself. Privately."

"And she knew about this?"

"No. She was only told that the adopting parents were a young couple who had personal reasons for wanting to remain anonymous."

"She doesn't know you took the boy to raise?"

Clay clenched his jaw. "No, and she's not going to. She didn't want him. She gave him away to the first person who asked for him. She doesn't deserve to know."

His dad leaned back in his chair, his expression grave. "You need to tell her. More importantly, you need to tell Eli. He thinks his mother died."

Clay bolted up. "No. Never. I'm not going to tell my son that his mother gave him up. That her *career* was more important than her child."

Dave clasped his hands. "What were her circumstances at the time?"

"I don't know." Clay rubbed his forehead. "She'd just gotten a job offer from some big news network. She was excited, but that's no excuse."

"Did you love her?"

"Yes, but that's not important."

"It is if you found yourself in this situation to begin with."

Clay looked away. Melody's announcement had been

a wake-up call to the life he'd been living. It had set him back on the right path, and he'd vowed to stay there. Well, with the exception of the falsehood around Eli's birth.

Dave sighed. "I suppose the easiest thing would be to let her go. Remove her from your life."

A rush of relief whooshed through Clay. "That would be—"

"But I'm not going to do that. You need to sort this out, Clay. Confront the past and uncover the truth so everyone can move forward from here honestly."

"I am not telling Eli who Melody is."

"Oh, and how do you plan on keeping it a secret?"

Clay shrugged. "I'll keep them apart. There's no reason for them to even meet."

Dave snorted. "It's a small town, Clay. Secrets are nearly impossible to keep. Especially when there's already curiosity about you and Eli's mother."

"I'll handle it."

"Are you going to work with her on this history project? I need to know."

Clay scratched his head, frustrated. "I'm not going to let you down, Dad. I know how important this is to you." He'd taken on this bicentennial job only because he loved the town so much. "Stop worrying. I'm an adult. I can handle this."

"I hope so."

Clay turned and walked to the door, but Dave wasn't done.

"Son, you can't live a lie," he said. "It always comes back to bite you. The truth will set you free."

"No, Dad. The truth will hurt the only person in the world I care about."

Clay drove back to the airfield on their property and parked near the hangar. His father didn't understand. There was nothing to be gained from telling Eli that his mother wasn't dead but was here in Blessing. There was nothing to gain in telling Melody either. Not that she'd care.

No. Best to keep the past in the past—right where it belonged. Let Melody do her job and be on her way. Surely, he could maintain a facade of cooperation for the few months she'd be here. All he had to do was put her in touch with the right people. The rest was up to her.

The quiet interior of her car was a welcome refuge the next morning and gave Melody time to settle down as she drove downtown and parked in the lot behind the annex. Chaos had reigned at Sandy's this morning as everyone got ready for work and school. She took a sip of her flavored coffee and tried not to think about what she would do if the Reynoldses let her go.

Her gaze traveled to the folder Dave Reynolds had given her. She'd taken some quiet time before everyone woke up this morning to look it over. The information had refueled her enthusiasm for the task. Blessing had a rich history, and she'd already come up with ideas for the layout of the book and started a list of possible sections. She was looking forward to taking pictures—if she got the opportunity and Clay didn't have her dismissed. She reminded herself that the Lord had brought her this far and He'd see her through the next phase, no matter what that might be.

Gathering up her belongings, she made her way inside to the small office she'd been assigned. Dave wasn't in his office and Clay was nowhere in sight. At least they weren't firing her first thing. She'd take the opportunity to visit the library and start gathering her research. Maybe if she dug right in, they wouldn't want to let her go.

The library wasn't hard to find. Perched on a slight rise, the stately former school building was surrounded by large live oaks. Like everything else in Blessing, it was loaded with charm.

The woman at the counter smiled brightly. "Oh, you must be the book lady."

Word traveled fast in Blessing. "I am."

"Miss Deborah is anxious to meet you. Let me get her."

A smiling woman in her late fifties emerged from the back, her gray hair styled in a neat pageboy and a chain with reading glasses hanging around her neck. "Miss Williams. I'm so pleased to meet you. I'm Deborah Wexler, the head librarian."

"Hello. I must admit I'm surprised you all recognized me already. I've only been here two days."

"We don't get many strangers in town, and we've been looking forward to you being here. Follow me. I have a stack of research materials you'll need."

It took a rolling cart to transfer the stack of books to Melody's car, and she drove back to her small office bubbling with excitement. Miss Deborah, as she insisted on being called, would be an invaluable resource. She'd already promised to start digging out old newspaper files and historical documents for Melody to look through. With the librarian's help, she might not have to call upon Clay much at all.

She made the final haul of books to her office and dumped the pile on the last empty spot of her tiny desk.

It was obvious that this space wouldn't work at all for the task ahead.

"I don't think we gave you a big enough office."

She jumped, then glanced over her shoulder as Dave walked in. "I had no idea you'd have this many resources already in print."

"Oh, you'll collect more before you're done." He laughed. "Many of our residents have written family histories that they'll want to share with you."

Melody set her hands on her hips and surveyed the crowded room. "Then I'll have to make room somehow."

"Can you work from home?"

"Oh, no. I'm staying with a friend. She has three kids in a tiny house. I'm sleeping on the hide-a-bed in the living room. But I plan on getting my own place as soon as I can find a free moment. The project will take several months, and I can't stay with Sandy that long."

"Hmm. That's not going to be easy. Blessing isn't a real estate hotbed." Dave frowned and tugged his ear. "You know, I think I might have a solution that will work out for both of us. I have a small cottage on our property. No one's lived in it since my mom passed two years ago. It's completely furnished. All it needs is a quick cleaning. Give me today to get the utilities turned on and someone to sweep the place out, and you can move in tomorrow."

"Oh, I don't want to be any trouble."

"Nonsense. We need to make this project as easy as possible for you."

A place of her own. It was exactly what she needed. However, living on the Reynoldses' homestead presented a new set of problems. What would Clay think of this arrangement? She could just imagine… She tugged on her sleeve.

On the other hand, if Dave was offering her a place to live, then she must still be employed.

"Dad."

She froze when she heard Clay's voice, bracing for the guillotine blade to fall, cutting her off from gainful employment.

"Morning, son. I just offered our book lady the cottage. It'll be more convenient for her since you'll be working together, and it's quiet and private. Just what she needs to assemble all the information she'll be collecting. Plus, she'll have access to your granddad's library. There's plenty of Blessing history in there."

Clay cleared his throat. "Whatever you think best." Melody could feel his disapproval like a fourth person in the room.

Dave patted his son's shoulder, then walked away.

Melody studied Clay. The hard tone in his deep voice had shocked her. He glanced her way, and his eyes were not the sky blue she remembered, but the steely blue she'd seen when she'd refused to give him an answer to his marriage proposal.

He leaned against the door frame, his jaw rigid, his body language closed and defensive. Just as he turned to go, she reached out and took his arm. The warmth of his skin brought back unwanted memories. He'd always been such a warm man—in heart and in nature.

She pulled her hand back, her insides quivering. "Thank you for not firing me."

He cleared his throat and his voice was odd sounding when he spoke.

"That was Dad's decision. He wants us to work together. But I have a full-time job, and this is my busy season. You'll be on your own."

"I'm good with that. I'm used to working alone."

"Yeah, as I recall, you prefer to be alone. No entanglements. No responsibilities."

His harsh tone stung. One of the things she'd loved about him was his deep, smooth voice. Now, each word was like a tiny shard of ice falling on her skin.

"Clay, we can't keep swiping at each other. We can't change the past. I have many regrets, but I can't undo them. Couldn't we start fresh and go forward from here?"

"I don't know. There's a lot to forget."

"I'm sorry. All I can say is that I'm not the same person I was back then. I've had some difficult times, and they've changed me."

"People don't change."

"You have. You used to be easygoing and lighthearted. One of the things I loved about you was your sense of humor. What happened to it?"

He stopped and stared ahead a long moment before facing her. "Difficult times." He turned and walked out.

She caught her breath at the mockery in his tone. Clearly, he was carrying a grudge against her. Not that she could blame him. Her heart ached. She'd never wanted to hurt him. Her actions had hurt her even more.

But what difficult times had he faced? The wife who'd died? Is that what had turned him from a warm and loving man into a hard-shelled crab?

Whatever it was, if they didn't reach some sort of truce soon, they'd both suffer. Beyond that, it would hurt the city of Blessing and the history she wanted to write. She turned back to the pile of books on her desk. She couldn't let that happen, if for no other reason than to justify Dave's faith in her.

* * *

Clay strode back to his dad's office, his pulse throbbing from the feel of Melody's hand on his arm. She shouldn't have touched him. She'd created a crack in the wall he'd thought was solid and impenetrable, and now he'd have to be twice as vigilant. It didn't help that his father kept complicating things.

"Dad, what were you thinking? I can't have her living in the cottage."

"Why not? If it were anyone else, you'd agree with me. It's the perfect location for her to work."

"Why are you doing this? I told you who she is."

His dad looked up at him with a stern expression. "You did, and maybe that's why I want her closer. She's my grandson's mother."

"She gave him up. She didn't want him. How's he going to feel if he finds that out?" Clay hadn't meant to raise his voice, but his emotions were too strong.

"I don't know." Dave crossed his arms over his chest. "How's he going to feel when he finds out his father has lied to him all his life? You need to resolve this thing between you and Melody. It's unhealthy."

Clay set his hands on his hips, unable to accept what he was hearing. "You're taking her side?"

"No. But there are two sides to every story, and I've only heard yours."

"It's the only one that matters. Eli is my son. Period."

Dave stood and came around his desk. "Look, if you can't work with Melody, I'll take you off the project and find someone who can."

"You know I'm the most qualified."

"Do I? Jeffrey Hollis has lived here his whole life.

He knows more about Blessing history than anyone else in town."

Clay pivoted on his heel to leave, but his father took his arm. "Son, you can't live like this, with all this anger and resentment. It'll destroy you."

"That already happened. I can't be destroyed a second time."

"And neither can she."

"What does that mean?"

"Have you taken a good look at her?"

"No." He hadn't. He'd been too afraid of the emotions and memories a close examination would unleash. He couldn't risk it. He knew his resistance for Melody was weak.

"She's pale. Fragile. I think she's been through some sort of trauma. There's a look in her eyes that reminds me of your uncle Paul. Something has broken her spirit, and I don't think she's fully recovered."

Uncle Paul suffered from post-traumatic stress disorder after two tours in the army. No, Dad was way off on this one.

"Trust me. Nothing can break this woman."

"I used to think that about you, too. But when you brought Eli home, you were a changed man. You'd lost part of yourself. Maybe Melody has, too. I think you need to step back and look a little closer at the situation."

Dad might have a valid point, but looking closely at Melody was way too risky. He had to maintain the shell around his heart if he was going to get through this book project.

Sunday morning dawned full of bright sun and temperatures in the low eighties. For Melody, it was a welcome change from Iowa, where it was still snowy, in early March. She'd never liked the cold—it was part of the reason she'd decided to attend the University of Georgia. And that's where she'd met Clay. They'd lived in the same small apartment complex and both were taking classes at UGA. It'd been the happiest time of her life. Until it ended.

She shook her head. *Stop it! That was then. This is now, and you're fine.*

With effort, she focused on her surroundings. Spring had already arrived in Blessing, and the town was a feast for the eyes. The trees were already leafing out, and everywhere she looked azalea bushes were bursting with colorful blossoms. The gentle breeze and the sunshine were the perfect antidote to her constant state of distress.

In the few days Melody had been in Blessing, she and Deborah, the librarian, had become good friends. When the older woman had invited her to attend church with her, she'd readily agreed. Her new life depended on her resting on God's grace and support every day, especially now, with Clay back in her life.

With a sigh, she pulled her car in behind Deborah's and climbed out. Her new friend's warm welcome buoyed Melody's spirits. Together, the women approached the front steps of the Blessing Community Church, just in time to meet Clay, Dave and a young boy walking in from the other direction.

Melody swallowed hard and tried to smile. She'd hoped for a quiet service, time to reflect and draw on the Word for the coming week. That would be difficult with Clay in the sanctuary.

The Reynolds men stopped and said good-morning.

Melody couldn't look away from the boy. He was all legs and arms, with a shock of wavy brown hair and bright blue eyes like his father and grandfather. Dave noticed her attention and made the introduction. "Melody, this is my grandson, Eli. Eli, Miss Melody is the book lady we've been talking about."

He raised his hand and grinned. "Hey."

"Nice to meet you, Eli." She glanced at Clay and her concern spiked. His blue eyes were stormy, and his mouth was pinched in a hard line. He held her gaze for only a moment, then steered his son toward the door.

"We'd better get inside."

The boy went ahead, his grandfather right behind, leaving Clay to walk beside her and Deborah. She searched for something to say. "He looks like you, Clay."

He stared at her a moment. "Thanks. He's a great kid."

Once inside, he moved off and joined his family. Melody and Deborah took seats at the back of the church.

Deborah leaned close. "Clay's a great dad," she confided. "He adores that boy."

No doubt. She'd always known he would be. "It must be hard raising a boy alone."

"Dave's a big help. They're a strong family."

Melody let herself be drawn into the service, smiling when the pastor referenced one of her favorite verses, a passage from Romans that spoke of God being the potter and having the right to create some things for noble purpose and others for common use. She used to think she'd been created for a noble purpose until He'd shown her that He had a more common use in mind.

She was okay with that. She just hadn't figured out what it was yet.

* * *

Melody turned onto the long driveway of the Reynoldses' homestead the next morning, her eyes widening at the impressive home situated at the edge of a large pond. Two large dormers graced the roof of the sprawling ranch-style farmhouse, and a porch ran the length of the front. Full-grown trees framed the home, and colorful blooming azaleas completed the picture. She hadn't imagined Clay growing up in a place like this, but it explained a lot about his values and character.

The driveway split, and following her directions, she took the fork to the left. She drove past a grove of trees and came to rest beside a small pale blue cottage. Her heart fluttered. She would love staying here. It was a dream cottage, and it was all her own.

Except—the only fly in the ointment was that she could see Clay's home easily from here.

Maybe, if she concentrated on her work, she wouldn't notice him coming or going.

She climbed out of the car and made her way to the porch. It'd be perfect for a rocking chair and a small table. Inside, the home was everything she could have hoped. Cozy but not cramped, furnished with lovingly worn furniture, and plenty of windows to let in the light. She walked through the small kitchen to a generous bedroom and bath. Finally, a second bedroom that would serve as an office completed the floor plan.

She grinned and clasped her hands, filled with happiness. Her first home. Not by ownership but by emotion.

Hurrying out to the car, she began bringing in boxes. Dave had offered to help her move in, but she'd assured him she had little to worry with. Other than her clothes, the stacks of research books were the only items she was bringing with her.

She was on her third trip to the car when she saw a boy riding up on his bike. She smiled when she realized it was Eli Reynolds.

"Hello."

"Hey. Grandpa said you'd be moving into my great-grandma's house."

"I am. It's a lovely cottage."

"Why are you coming here?"

There was no challenge in his tone, only curiosity. "I have a lot of work to do, and your grandpa thought this would be a nice, quiet place for me to get it done."

"What kind of work?"

"I'm writing a book about Blessing's history."

"Oh. I thought when he said you were the book lady you might write superhero adventure books."

His disappointed expression made her smile. "Maybe next time. You know, there are all kinds of heroes in history."

He shrugged. She moved to the front seat of her car and pulled out the bag that held her camera gear.

"What's that?"

"My photo equipment."

"You take pictures?"

"I do. I'll be taking lots of them for the book while I'm here."

He straddled his bike, rolling it back and forth as he watched. "I wish I had a camera."

"Do you like taking pictures?"

"I guess. Do you?"

"Very much." She pulled her old Nikon from the bag. "This is my favorite."

"Whoa." His blue eyes widened. "That's awesome."

Melody started to show him how it worked, but the sound of a fast-approaching vehicle drew their attention. The black pickup skidded to a halt behind Melody's car. Her heart chilled when an angry Clay emerged.

"Eli. Go back to the house."

"I wanted to meet the book lady. She has cool cameras."

Clay gestured toward the house. "Grandpa needs you. Get going."

"Yes, sir."

The boy glanced at Melody. "See ya."

"Goodbye, Eli. It was nice talking to you. Come back anytime, and I'll show you all my photography gear."

Clay stood wooden and stoic until his son was well away from the cottage.

"I don't want you inviting Eli over here."

"I didn't. He just came over." She crossed her arms over her chest and faced him. "But why not? He's a nice boy. Friendly, like you used to be."

His jaw flexed. "He has chores and schoolwork. And you have a big project. I don't want him distracted or distracting you."

"Clay, what harm could it do?"

Without answering, he climbed back into his truck and drove away.

She watched him leave, confusion on her face. *Does he really hate me so much he won't even let his son talk to me?* She had to find a way to deal with the man. This constant stress wouldn't help her work.

She just didn't know how to achieve that.

Clay sat down at the table and took a bite of the roast beef his father had fixed for supper. He was glad Dad liked to cook because it wasn't a skill he'd acquired—unless it involved a grill or a smoker.

"How was your day, Big E?" Dave gently punched Eli's shoulder.

"Good. I got a hundred on the math quiz. And I got to meet the book lady again."

"Her name is Miss Melody," Dave corrected.

"Yes, sir. She had a big bag of cameras. It was awesome."

"Really. Well, maybe she can show you how to take some cool pictures."

Clay jabbed at a piece of beef on his plate. "I don't think he should bother Miss Melody. She has a lot of work to do."

His dad gave him a stern look. Clay shrugged. No sense trying to hide his motives. Dad knew the real reason behind his comment.

But he didn't leave it alone. "Oh, I don't know," he said. "She's new here. She might like to have a friend to visit her now and again."

"I liked her. She was nice."

Dave smiled. "I agree. I think she's nice, too."

Clay couldn't ignore the challenge in his father's tone.

Eli reached for a dinner roll. "I think she's lonely, though."

"What makes you say that?" Dave asked.

Eli shrugged. "She has a sad smile."

Dave nodded. "Then we should all try to make her feel welcome, don't you think?"

Clay held his tongue until he and his dad were alone. "I don't want Eli getting close to Melody."

His dad turned to face him, pinning him with the

look Clay knew meant that he should pay attention to the advice he was about to receive.

"Then the worst thing you can do is forbid him to spend time with her. It'll only encourage him to sneak away to visit her. Is that what you want?"

"No, but—"

"If a ten-year-old kid can see that Melody is vulnerable, why can't a thirty-three-year-old grown man?" Then he walked off, leaving Clay feeling as if he were the ten-year-old.

Unfortunately, Dad had a point. He had to find a way to set aside his anger toward Melody. It was exhausting and went against his nature. He was generally compassionate and understanding toward others. In fact—and ironically, really—his history with Melody was what had given him a better understanding of others' loss and pain.

So why couldn't he afford her the same grace?

A Bible verse flashed into his mind. *Blessed are the merciful for they shall receive mercy.*

Maybe it was time for some serious introspection. Melody's sudden appearance in his life had created an emotional case of fifty-two-card pickup, and it was time to start putting things in order.

Chapter Three

Clay steered his pickup through downtown and out Morrison Road the next day. Try as he might, he couldn't shake his father's observations about Melody. They'd rattled around in his mind all night until he couldn't evade them any longer. He'd been deliberately avoiding looking too closely at Melody, but now he wondered what Dad saw that he might have missed. And Eli, too.

He thought back over their few encounters, but each one was shrouded in a fog of anger. The only one that was partially clear was the moment the other day when she'd touched his arm. He'd looked into her eyes and seen something different. They were missing a remembered sparkle that had brightened her golden-brown eyes like an internal fire. The light had dimmed. There was a sadness in those eyes that he'd never seen before.

Melody had never been sad. Even when she talked about her difficult upbringing as a foster child, she'd maintained a positive and upbeat outlook on life. She'd had plans, dreams and ambitions.

He breathed a sigh of relief as he pulled into the parking lot of the Blessing Bridge. It was vacant. He wasn't sure why he'd come here. He did most of his praying early in the morning, fishing at the pond in front of the house. It was quiet and peaceful. Time there allowed him an opportunity to reset his attitude and emotions.

Today, however, he'd needed something more. Melody's appearance in his life had knocked him off-kilter and had him questioning his direction. He might have managed to control his emotions enough to work with her on the book—after all, she'd be doing most of the work on her own. But having her live in the cottage, only a few yards away, would mean he'd see her every move. Worse, Eli would be exposed to her daily. Clay's stomach tightened at the thought.

He made his way down the shaded path, stepping over broken branches and tree roots as he went. The park commission had made an offer to buy the bridge land outright. They wanted to clean up the area and landscape at least for the bicentennial next year, but they were meeting with significant resistance. They did the best they could keeping the path clear, but they depended on volunteers and sometimes they fell behind on the task.

The owner felt the easement he'd allowed was all he needed to do. He had no desire to lease or sell the bridge portion of his land to the city of Blessing. The city council was in the process of forming a committee to look deeper into the situation. The easement expired in a few months, and they were worried that the owner wouldn't renew their agreement. Without the bridge, the bicentennial would be missing its primary attraction.

Clay's footsteps thudded loudly on the wooden deck of the old bridge as he walked to the middle. Below him, the water in the large pond rippled as a duck waddled along at the edge.

He searched for words to pray. Nothing came to mind. It was hard to pray with sincerity when your mind and heart were filled with anger and resentment. He knew his father was right. He needed to let go of the past, but Eli's happiness and his future were at stake. There was no reason to change his decision. It had worked well for over ten years.

Dad's assessment of Melody nagged at his mind. He'd said she was fragile. Clay tried to remember the way she'd looked when they were together, but all he could recall was the play of emotions over her features when he'd asked her to marry him. She'd looked shocked, then afraid, and then her eyes had filled with iron-willed determination.

He'd been tempted many times over the years to search her name on the internet, but he'd always changed his mind. He didn't want to learn that she'd achieved success as an international correspondent by giving up her child.

A bird startled him, squawking as it took flight from the brush. But if she had, why wasn't she working as a journalist? Why had she taken a low-paying job compiling the history of a small Southern town? A job she'd said she needed. Why?

What had happened to her? She'd told him that life had been difficult and she'd changed. So maybe he should at least give her the benefit of the doubt. He could declare a truce. It would be the most practical approach.

This book project didn't concern only him. The whole town was involved. Getting along with Melody would benefit everyone. Besides, the sooner he cooperated, the sooner she'd be gone. And if he helped, maybe she'd even finish the book ahead of schedule.

He was halfway back toward his car before he realized he hadn't actually prayed at all. He'd only found a new way to protect his secret.

Melody flipped a page in the family history booklet Mrs. Victor Bettencourt had brought her. Written in cursive with a quill pen, it was difficult to read, but Melody was determined to decipher the faded script. It would prove invaluable to the overall story of Blessing, she was sure. This kind of thing fueled her enthusiasm for the project.

"Good morning."

Melody pulled her attention from the faded pages. "Clay." *What are you doing here?* After his warning yesterday about Eli staying away, she'd expected him to avoid her like the plague.

"I stopped by the cottage, but you weren't there. I didn't expect to find you back in this cramped office."

She smiled. "Turns out it's a perfect place to meet with the locals to discuss their contributions to the book. Mrs. Bettencourt came by this morning and left me some family papers."

A grin moved Clay's lips, and Melody's heart flipped. It was the first smile she'd seen from him since she'd arrived in Blessing, and it unleashed memories of the man she'd fallen in love with.

"I'm not surprised. She's the chairwoman of the historical society."

"So she said." Melody paused, her emotions braced for another angry encounter.

"Are you free for a while?"

"Yes." What was he up to?

"I thought I could give you that tour of downtown Blessing we never got around to. I know it would help you get a better feel for the community."

She hadn't expected that. Maybe he was kidding. "Aren't you afraid you'll get cooties or something if you spend too much time with me?"

He chuckled. She blinked, unsure she'd heard right.

"I have some anti-cootie pills in my pocket."

Melody's heart started to melt. This was the Clay she remembered. *No.* She stiffened. Now she was really on her guard. "What's this about, Clay? Why the sudden switch to Mr. Nice Guy?"

He shrugged and hooked his thumbs into his jeans pockets. "You were right. We can't keep growling at each other. You have a job to do that will benefit my hometown. It would be best for both of us if we called a truce. I thought I'd make the first move since you're the guest here. A tour of Blessing would be helpful to you. What do you say? I'm the perfect guide. I know everything and everyone."

She frowned, studying his expression. Was he sincere? He had a point. She could learn only so much from books and documents. She needed to connect with the town if she was going to write a book that would touch the hearts of its residents. "All right. When?"

"Now. It's a beautiful day."

"Okay." She walked with him to the front door of the annex, keeping her guard up. He let her exit first, then stopped and surveyed the downtown landscape.

"Which direction do you want to start?"

Downtown Blessing was formed around a central square, anchored on one end by the historic courthouse and by the hundred-year-old First Church of Blessing on the other.

"I think we'll cover it all, so it doesn't matter."

"Good point."

They started down the sidewalk, away from the courthouse on the north end of the square. Clay began a running commentary on each building, its origin and owners. Each storefront added to her fascination for the town. The few empty buildings sparked her imagination, too. She stopped in front of an old theater. "Is this still in use?"

Clay shook his head, staring up at the tall Palace sign that had become faded and broken over time. "No. It's been closed for several years. Too expensive to restore."

"Why are you doing this, Clay? Really."

He took a moment to respond. "You're going to be here for several months. Stomping around angry about something I can't change is a waste of time. What about you? Why are you here in an obscure Southern town, working on an even more obscure little book?"

Was this his motive? To dig out her past? Fine. She could tell him all about it. Up to a point.

"I discovered I wasn't cut out for the international scene. So I came back home."

"To write small-town history books?"

"No. I'm trying out new things. Looking for a new direction."

"How did you even find out about this job?"

"Sandra Hackett, my foster sister, lives here in Blessing. She told me about it."

"Oh, I know Sandy. She taught Eli's Sunday school class. Nice lady. So she's the sister you used to talk about?"

She hadn't realized she'd talked about her past that much when she and Clay were dating. "Yes. What about you? Did you ever start your own business like you wanted?"

"No. When I came home, I had a new perspective on things. I decided to go to work in the family business instead."

"Oh? Politics?"

"No. We own an agricultural application business."

She stopped and faced him. "What's that?"

He raised his eyebrows. "Crop dusting."

Melody couldn't stop her smile. "You mean you're a hotshot daredevil air jockey who swoops low over the fields and terrorizes the locals?"

Her tease set his jaw into flexing mode again. What had she said? Apparently, his sense of humor wasn't fully restored.

"You should try to keep current, Miss Williams. That old image of crop dusters died out with the Prohibition. Modern-day crop application is a highly skilled and technical profession."

He was serious.

"I'm sorry. I just never thought of you flying back and forth over cornfields."

"Stop by the airstrip tomorrow, and I'll give you a quick lesson in agricultural application techniques and the technology required to make it possible."

"I'd like that. Wait—the sign I saw at the end of your driveway, Dusty Birds. Is that your company?"

"Yes. It's a third-generation business. The largest in the tricounty area."

"And you fly the planes?" She'd never thought of him as a pilot but looking at him now, she could easily see him in the cockpit. His boy-next-door good looks were poster perfect for the job.

"All three of them. Not at the same time, of course."

Her heart sank. How had she not known this about him? Probably because she'd been too busy looking to her future. "I'm sorry. I didn't remember this."

"Don't beat yourself up. We didn't talk much about who we were before we met. We were too busy enjoying each other. All that mattered was being in the moment."

"You're right. I never wanted to think about anything beyond the moment."

Melody started walking, too uncomfortable to stand still. They walked in silence for a while, then crossed over to the park in the middle of the square. Clay stopped next to a large statue of a soldier. The plaque on the stand gave his name as Sergeant Linwood Croft, hero of the First World War who had heroically saved his platoon by taking out a German machine-gun bunker.

"This is amazing. The town must be proud of its native son."

"He's revered around here. One of the top three bragging points for Blessing. The bridge, Sergeant Croft and Riverbank Park."

"I'll be sure to devote space to honoring your local hero."

Clay's cell phone rang. He pulled it from his pocket and excused himself to walk away. When he rejoined her, there was a frown on his face.

"Is everything all right?"

"It will be. One of our customers has taken his business to our competitor. The second one this week."

"Sounds serious."

He shrugged. "It just means I'll have to work a little harder."

Clay resumed his role as tour guide, and they made their way around the square. They finished by taking the walkway down to the river park and strolling beside the calm waters.

"This is lovely. Very peaceful." The winding path was complemented by planters overflowing with flowers and interspersed with benches. On the opposite bank, the ground sloped gently, a green carpet dotted with picnic tables and shelters.

"This is one of the last things my dad accomplished before he left office," Clay said. "He was mayor of Blessing for over twenty years. He wanted to beautify the waterfront. It was turning into a muddy, dangerous hangout for gangs."

"You must be very proud."

"My dad is a good man. He cares deeply for Blessing and its citizens. It's why he ran for city council even though he'd retired from his mayoral duties. This bicentennial is really important to him."

"What about you?"

He shrugged. "I agreed to help because I'd do anything for him."

That was the Clay she'd fallen in love with. Kind, compassionate and caring. Had losing his wife robbed him of those qualities? She wanted to ask him about her, but their truce was too new and fragile. She'd wait for a better time.

Clay's guided tour of downtown Blessing proved to be invaluable. He introduced her to many of the merchants on the square, pointed out the first building constructed in the town and described the lean times after the Civil War. He told her how the town had struggled to keep from dying out. He talked about the boom years when lumber was king and the wealth it had brought to the town. Then he touched lightly on more recent history—the closing of several factories, the fire that had severely damaged the courthouse and the tornado four years ago that had destroyed many of the ancient live oaks around the town, a point of pride the citizens still mourned.

Each point of interest kicked her enthusiasm up another notch and made her more determined to do a good job. Her head was spinning with ideas when they returned to the annex.

Clay slipped his hands into his pockets. "Have you learned enough about Blessing? Or did I overload you with too much information?"

"Oh, no. It was wonderful, actually very helpful. I'm looking forward to talking with people about their family's contributions. Hearing their personal stories is going to be fascinating. This book might be bigger than we anticipated."

"I'll see if we can enlarge the budget."

As Melody stepped up to the door, her toe caught on the concrete. She stumbled, and Clay grasped her left arm. She winced and pulled away.

"Are you okay?"

She nodded, suddenly realizing how tired she was. The tour had been exhilarating but it had also taxed her stamina. "I'm just tired. You were right. That was a lot of information to process in one afternoon. I think I'll go home and start making notes."

"Maybe you should rest."

She shook her head. "Can't accomplish anything that

way." His eyes narrowed and he studied her, making her uneasy.

"Thanks again for the tour." The words rushed out in an effort to distract him.

"That's what I'm here for. If you have questions or need information on something specific, just ask. If I don't know the answer, I'm sure I know someone who does."

"I'll hold you to that. I'm glad we're working together now."

"Yeah. Me, too."

Melody watched him disappear around the corner of the building toward the parking lot, then made her way inside to her office. Fatigue drained her last reserves. She needed to rest. Gathering up her notes from the meeting with Mrs. Bettencourt, she headed home, eager to settle down inside her little cottage and sort through the events of the day.

She didn't know what had made Clay change his mind about working together. He'd only said they needed to set the past aside for the good of everyone. She had a feeling there was more to it than that, but whatever his reason, she was happy and relieved. She'd be looking at several long and unpleasant months ahead without it. This would be so much easier and fun, working with him instead of against him.

Relaxing in her cozy living room, she took a bite of a cookie she'd purchased when they'd stopped at Blair's Bakery on the square.

Clay had been like the man she remembered. Almost. She'd sensed he was still holding back and still not happy she was there, but the anger and resentment were gone. Or at least masked. Time would tell. She appreciated his kindness, but it had created a new wrinkle. Ten years ago, she'd been in love with him. If he kept behaving like his old self, she was in grave danger of falling for him again. And that would be disastrous. Even if they could become friends again, anything else was out of the question. Nothing could change what she'd done to him. Nothing could bring back the baby she'd given up.

The two biggest mistakes in her life.

Clay cast his line back into the pond, smiling down as Lady Bug, the family's Brittany spaniel, lumbered up beside him. Lady had delivered a litter of pups a few weeks ago, and this was the first time she'd joined him since. He'd missed her company in the morning while he fished. He glanced down at her. "Shouldn't you be with your babies?"

She tilted her head as if to say, "I needed a break. Those kids are all over me."

Clay gave her a scratch behind the ears, then turned his attention back to the line in the water. His gaze drifted to the cottage partially visible in the grove of trees.

This morning the cool breeze and calm water weren't having their usual soothing effect.

His tour with Melody yesterday had opened his eyes to many things he couldn't explain or understand. Dad kept insisting that Melody seemed fragile. Eli claimed she had a sad smile. He'd dismissed them both as nonsense, but now he was realizing their observations weren't so farfetched. Melody was different.

She'd started the tour happy and eager, but as they'd gone on, he'd noticed her slowing down. She'd taken several opportunities to sit on a bench, claiming she wanted to soak in the view and wishing she'd brought her camera.

She'd eagerly greeted each merchant and resident he'd introduced her to, but as they'd made their way around the square, her enthusiasm had waned. And then there was that stumble when they'd returned to the annex.

He'd taken a closer look, comparing her with the woman he'd met and fallen in love with years ago. Her auburn hair then had been shorter and wavy. Now it was long and straight, usually tied at the base of her neck. She'd always been fashionably dressed, yet now she favored plain pants and long-sleeved shirts.

There was a sadness to her smile and a brittle quality to her that he couldn't ignore. It was almost like, if she were pushed too hard, she might shatter into pieces. Concern knotted in the center of his chest. What had happened to her? Was she ill? A cancer survivor perhaps?

He cast his line into the water again, brushing aside his observations. He was probably just under the power of suggestion, taking what Dad and Eli had said too seriously.

This Melody was older and more mature. Of course she wasn't the same happy-go-lucky young woman he'd known. But she'd been so full of life and eager for each new experience. Now she seemed subdued, a pale version of the woman he remembered.

And he still didn't know why she was here. Why she'd have taken this little job. She'd said she needed it; she'd practically begged him not to fire her that first day. But she was an extremely intelligent woman who could accomplish whatever she decided to do. She'd possessed a never-give-up kind of drive. What had happened to her dreams? To her?

"And why do you care?" The words burst out, startling even himself in the early morning stillness.

He reached down for more bait to attach to his hook and caught sight of his son walking across the lawn. With Melody. His jaw clenched. This is what he'd been afraid of. He had to keep Eli and Melody apart. They couldn't get close.

By the time he collected his fishing gear and returned to the house, Eli and Melody had disappeared. He heard soft giggles coming from the garage as he drew closer.

"They're so adorable."

He stepped into the storage room and froze. Melody was sitting on the floor, cradling a small puppy to her chest and smiling as the other five pups tumbled around her. Eli sat cross-legged, telling her about each little animal.

Then she glanced up at Clay, and his heart stopped. For a moment, he saw the woman he'd fallen in love with. Her eyes were bright, her smile sweet. Her whole being glowed with life.

"What are you doing here?" He spoke the words without thinking. The light in Melody's eyes dimmed.

He really needed to watch his tone when he spoke to her. His old resentment kept leaking through.

"Hey, Dad!" Eli jumped up to give him a quick hug. "I wanted Miss Melody to see Lady's puppies."

"Who can resist puppies?" Melody smiled as she spoke, but her eyes watched Clay carefully.

He yanked his wandering memories back in check. "Eli. Don't you have chores to see to?"

"Yes, sir. But I can do them later."

"Go get started on them now."

"Why?"

"Eli."

"Yes, sir." He stood.

Melody smiled at his son. "Thank you for letting me see the puppies, Eli. That was very thoughtful of you."

"You're welcome."

Clay watched his son walk back to the house, then turned to face Melody. She'd placed the puppy back down with the others and was facing him. Her light brown eyes were dark.

"What is your problem?"

"I told you. I don't want you distracting Eli from his responsibilities."

"For the record, I didn't do any distracting. He stopped by the cottage to say hello and invite me to come and see the puppies. I accepted. I guess this means our truce is over?"

Clay rubbed his forehead, fighting to corral his surging anxiety and regain his footing. He had to remember Dad's warning. If he made too big a deal about keeping Melody and Eli apart, it would only drive them together. And he had declared a truce.

He cleared his throat. "No. We're good. Sorry. Like I said, I just want him to learn to be responsible." But it was a lame excuse, and they both knew it.

"I'm sure he will be, and I'm sure my being here won't change that in the slightest." She started from the garage. "But, Clay, I like Eli. He's a nice boy, and I'm not going to turn him away if he comes by the cottage just because you have a helicopter-parent notion that he should have his nose in his books and chores every moment."

She strode off, leaving Clay regretting his reaction and knowing he'd made things worse. He'd just wiped out any goodwill they'd gained from their tour. He'd hoped to take a step forward but instead had taken two steps back.

But it wasn't fair. He hadn't been prepared for the sight of Melody, sweet and smiling, cuddling a little dog. It had pushed open the door to his heart a little too far. He had to get it closed fast.

And padlocked.

Chapter Four

Melody reached for another book from the tall stack and opened the cover. Her tension had eased a good bit over the last two days, thanks to Clay's truce. Things were still a bit awkward but nothing like those first few days. Clay had kept his distance. Unfortunately, so had Eli and she regretted that. She'd looked forward to getting to know the boy better and perhaps finding a way for him to help with the book. He was curious and eager, but she doubted Clay would agree to him getting involved.

Turning her attention back to her work, she delved into the history of Burton and Naomi Bower, whose family had opened the first general store in Blessing. An hour later she stretched her back to work out the kinks then stood and fixed a glass of sweet tea, a new habit she'd acquired since coming to the South. Carrying it to the front porch, she sat on the step, reminding herself to hunt down a rocker in her next free moment. Her gaze scanned the soothing scene before her. Early green leaves budding out on the trees, splashes of color from the azaleas, daffodils and irises springing up in the flower beds—they were a sight to behold. She closed her eyes and inhaled the clean, fresh air. A low buzz overhead drew her attention. A small yellow plane soared through the blue sky. Was Clay at the controls or his dad?

Over the last several days she'd become accustomed to hearing the crop-dusting planes coming and going from the airstrip on the Reynoldses' land. She hadn't taken Clay up on his offer to check out the airplanes yet, but she planned to do so soon. The Reynolds family tree played a large role in the history of Blessing, and she wanted to be sure she did it justice.

A tiny bark interrupted her thoughts. She glanced down to see one of Lady's puppies staring up at her. He placed his paws on the bottom step and tried to climb up, but his legs weren't long enough yet. She giggled at the adorable sight and scooped him up, cuddling him close. "What are you doing over here, little guy? You're a long way from your brothers and sisters."

"He's the adventurous one of the litter. I find him wandering off all the time. Sorry about this."

Melody smiled as Clay came toward her. "No problem. I like it. He's so cute." She held the puppy close to her cheek.

"Maybe he'd like to stay here with you. He seems to head this direction whenever he escapes the garage."

"Really? I would love to have him stay with me when he's ready to leave his mama."

"He's ready now. If you're serious, he's yours."

"Thank you, Clay." She hugged the squirmy little dog. "I'll have to give you a name, won't I? You'll need a bed and food and bowls…" The idea filled her with excitement. "Is there a pet store in Blessing?"

Clay nodded and lowered himself onto the step beside her. "Perfect Pets. One block off the square on Chandler Street."

"I'm beginning to love your town."

"Good. I think they love you, too. I hear people talking about you all the time."

She smiled. At least the locals liked her. "All good, I hope. I'm looking forward to meeting more of the residents. Everyone so far has been so sweet and helpful."

"I'm glad to hear that because I have an invitation for you. It's the first of a series of monthly events celebrating the bicentennial. We're kicking things off with a porch crawl in the historic district. It'll be a good way for you to meet more of our citizens."

Melody wasn't sure she'd heard him right. "A what?"

He chuckled and reached over to scratch behind the puppy's ear. "It's like a progressive dinner. People stroll from house to house. Each home offers refreshments set out on their front porch. You stop, visit, eat a few goodies, then move on to the next porch. It's really a lot of fun."

The idea intrigued her, though she wasn't as comfortable with small talk as she used to be. However, she would be working, so it would give her an opportunity to ask questions and listen to family stories, which would require little small talk. "It sounds interesting and elegant. I'll look forward it. When and where should I report?"

"It's this Saturday at noon. I can pick you up a little before that."

Melody's enthusiasm for the event dimmed a few notches. Despite their truce, spending time alone with Clay still made her uneasy. She wasn't sure she wanted to spend an entire afternoon with him, but she couldn't attend without him either.

Clay noticed her hesitation. "If you'd rather not take part in the crawl, there's a family picnic taking place at Riverbank Park."

Melody considered that option but decided the crawl would be the more comfortable choice. "I have to admit the porch crawl intrigues me."

He smiled. "I think you'll enjoy it. You might get two or three more chapters for the book."

"That would be wonderful. Though I'm collecting so much history I'm not sure I can finish this book on schedule."

"If anybody can, you can. You're the most determined woman I've ever known."

She wasn't sure if that was a slur or a compliment. "Is that a good thing?"

He met her gaze, his blue eyes clouded. "Most of the time."

The puppy barked and Melody set him down. He scampered off a ways and sniffed a branch on the ground. It would be nice having a puppy in the house. She could use some companionship.

"Have you picked a name yet?" Clay asked.

"I'm thinking about Barney."

He shrugged. "As good as any I suppose."

"You don't like it?"

"I do if you do." He stood.

She rose. "I guess your dad is flying today? I heard a plane overhead earlier."

Clay shook his head. "My full-timer, Jared Miller, is flying today. My dad doesn't take the controls anymore. He suffered a minor stroke a while back and decided he shouldn't be in the cockpit anymore. I was proud of him for doing that. But that's when he decided to run for city council."

"Being in charge of a big event like a bicentennial sounds like a lot of stress."

"It is, but it's safer. If he has another episode, it'd better to be behind a desk than flying a hundred and fourteen miles an hour three feet above the ground."

"Good point. So you and Jared are the pilots now?"

Clay nodded. "We have a part-timer, Greg Zachary, who fills in when we're at peak season."

Melody studied Clay a moment, judging his mood. He appeared relaxed and open, so maybe he would be receptive to her suggestion.

"Clay, I was wondering if you would allow Eli to help me with the book in his spare time. He could sort through the pictures and keep the family histories together."

Clay's shoulders stiffened as his shield shot into place. "Maybe you need an assistant. Someone qualified."

"No. I just need someone to keep things straightened up at the end of the day. Eli would be perfect for the job. I could pay him, unless you object."

Clay rubbed his chin. "I'll have to think about it. His school and chores come first."

"Yes, I know." Barney scampered back and barked. Melody scooped him up and held him close. She turned to Clay with a smile, but his expression wiped it from her face. He was frowning, his blue eyes narrowed. What had she done now?

He stood abruptly. "I have a lot of work today. I'll see you this weekend." And with that, he strode away.

"Goodbye to you, too," Melody muttered under her breath. She shook her head. She'd never understand his odd mood changes. One minute he was warm and friendly, the next all cold and distant.

Barney squirmed and Melody giggled. "We need to get you some puppy gear, little guy."

She also had an appointment with a local to discuss their family contributions to Blessing. Might as well kill two birds, so to speak. She could use a long talk with Sandy, too. It was time for a sister-to-sister discussion. Maybe she could shed some light on Clay's odd behavior.

Every encounter with him left her feeling off-balance and shut out.

Melody hurried down the sidewalk on Church Street a short while later, catching sight of Sandy seated at an outdoor table in front of the Blue Bird Café. It was the first chance they'd had to have lunch together in nearly a week, and she desperately needed to talk to her sister.

Sandy reached for Melody's hand as she sat down. "I'm so glad you suggested this. I've missed you since you moved into the cottage."

"Me, too. I keep meaning to call, but I'm up to my elbows in research."

"And loving every moment of it. Except, I'm guessing, for working with Clay."

She nodded. "We've declared a truce, but it's shaky at best. That's what I wanted to talk to you about. I thought since you've lived here so long, you might know something that could help me understand him."

"Not really. I've only been here five years. I can tell

you the rumors I've heard, but that's not exactly reliable. Things get embellished and distorted in a small town."

"I suppose." She took a sip of her drink.

"I wasn't here, but from what I've been told, Clay came home one day with a baby and explained that the mother died. No one ever met her. He doesn't talk about her, but everyone's always assumed that's just because it's too painful for him." She laughed. "When you say it that way, it's sounds weird, doesn't it? But everyone I know thinks highly of him. He takes care of his dad, he adores his son, and he's an honest and honorable man."

Melody sighed. "All of which I knew. I guess he's still holding a grudge for the way I left. I should have at least given him an answer to his proposal. At the time, all I could think about was getting away."

"I understand. Getting away from things was how we dealt with a crisis. As foster kids, no one ever taught us how to stand and face adversity."

The truth of that statement lodged uncomfortably in her chest. "No, they didn't. Though Mama Kay tried." Thoughts of their mutual foster mother made her smile. "I'll never be able to repay her for what she's done for me."

"For us. We both could have ended up down very different paths. She was truly a blessing. She gave me the courage to go to college to become a teacher."

Melody nodded. "She brought me to faith and gave me a refuge when I needed it most. I don't know what I would have done if she hadn't taken me in when I got pregnant."

Sandy smiled. "I tried to get her to move down here and be the kids' surrogate grandmother, but she didn't want to leave Des Moines. Not even the warmer climate could persuade her."

"She's rooted there, I'm afraid."

The waitress brought their food and placed it on the table.

Melody turned her thoughts to the next topic she wanted to discuss.

"I wanted to ask you about an event I'm going to tomorrow. A porch crawl."

A big smile appeared on Sandy's face. "Oh, you'll love it. It's very elegant and quintessentially Southern. What are you going to wear?"

Melody set down her fork and frowned, a small lump of concern forming in her throat. "Wear? Is there a dress code for a porch crawl?"

Sandy laughed. "No, but I don't think your usual jeans and cotton shirt will do. You'll be meeting the old guard of Blessing. You should at least wear a skirt or dress."

Melody mentally scrolled through the items in her closet. Jeans, pants, several long-sleeved cotton shirts and two long-sleeved knit ones more suitable for church. "I don't own a dress."

"I was hoping you'd say that." Sandy rubbed her hands together and grinned. "I think we need a shopping trip and maybe a visit to Tresses Beauty Shop."

"Are you suggesting a makeover?"

"Was I too subtle?" Sandy patted her arm. "You'll be with Clay and meeting our most prominent citizens. You need to look the part."

Melody squirmed. "I'm not going to this event to impress anyone. I'm going to ask questions."

"And they might be more forthcoming if you look

a little more, um…" She waved her finger in a circle. "Professional."

Melody glanced down at her faded jeans and tennis shoes. Sandy had a point. "I wouldn't know where to begin."

"I do. I have the rest of the afternoon free and as soon as we finish our lunch, we're going to get you all dolled up for tomorrow."

"I'm not sure I want to be dolled up."

Sandy frowned. "You really have changed. Shopping used to be your favorite thing in the world. You were super aware of your appearance every moment."

"That's before the world changed me."

"Yeah, well… I want to get some of that old Melly back. It'll do wonders for your attitude and self-esteem."

Melody sighed. Once Sandy made up her mind, there was no changing it. She was like a little terrier. But the idea did sound fun.

Sandy marched her down the block to a boutique on the town square called Forrest Fashions. The owner, Camille Forrest, helped her select a pale blue dress suitable for the balmy spring weather of Mississippi. The dress was short-sleeved, so Melody added a lightweight long-sleeved jacket to wear over it.

After selecting a pair of low-heeled sandals, Sandy escorted her to Tresses, the beauty shop around the corner, and delivered her into the hands of Mildred Graham. Before Melody knew it, her long locks were transformed to a modern chin-length style that floated softly around her face when she moved. Then Mildred insisted she let the manicurist do her nails and gave her a pale pink color that looked like spring.

Melody gauged her reflection in the mirror, realizing she'd neglected her personal appearance for too long. Looking good hadn't been a priority lately.

Sandy smiled and clapped her hands when Melody met her at The Grind, a coffee shop on the square. "You look fantastic! I knew Mildred would do wonders with you."

Melody touched her fingers to her hair. "I do feel lighter and more confident." She had to admit it felt good to be free of the long strands. Thanks to a natural wave, this style would require little to no maintenance. She felt like a new woman. Almost.

"Good. It's time you started letting go of the past and rejoin the present."

Sandy was right. She'd withdrawn from the world after the explosion. Rejoining life had been harder than she'd ever anticipated. "I know. I'm working on it. That's why I took this job. I hoped it would rebuild my confidence."

Sandy patted her hand. "I believe it will. I know the good Lord brought you here for a reason, and I'm so grateful that He did."

"I don't know about that, but I'm glad I came. For the most part."

"Hang in there, sis." Sandy took her hands in a warm embrace. "Be patient. Remember, this is on God's schedule, not yours."

It was good advice, but Melody wasn't sure she could abide by it. Not while things between her and Clay were so unsettled.

Then again, she had no choice. She'd learned that

God's plans were always on a different timetable from her own, but they always worked out for the better.

Melody was failing badly with her patience. Clay was due any moment, and her nerves were vibrating on full alert. She should never have agreed to attend the porch crawl with him. She caught a glimpse of herself in the bedroom mirror, and her nerves jumped up a notch. Her new look was making things worse. The change was too drastic. Would he think the makeover was for his benefit? She spun away from her image. Ridiculous. He could barely disguise his resentment toward her. He could not care less what she looked like.

Anyway, it was too late to change her mind. A knock on the door announced Clay's arrival. All she could do now was go through the event and hope for the best.

She pasted on a smile and opened the door. Clay blinked and stared a long moment. "Wow. I wouldn't have recognized you. You look like you did back when—"

He stopped speaking, and she looked down at the floor, overwhelmingly self-conscious. "Am I over-dressed? Sandy said this would be more appropriate than jeans and a top. It's been a long time since I wore anything feminine." Her cheeks flamed and she resisted the urge to cover her face with her palms. Clay had no interest in her wardrobe habits.

He smiled. "I just meant you look nice. Very nice."

"Thank you."

"Shall we go?" He gestured toward the door, and she walked ahead of him, remembering the times they'd spent together, following whatever whim captured their fancy that day. But that was then. Today was about meeting the townspeople, making connections that would aid in making this book the best it could be.

Clay opened the car door for her, and she settled in, clutching her purse and her camera in her lap. She kept her gaze on the scenery as they drove through town and onto a wide boulevard lined with huge live oaks and large homes nestled on green lawns. The middle of the avenue was laid out like a long park with a winding walkway and welcoming benches along the way.

Vehicles lined the street, and Clay pulled into the last remaining parking spot. Melody exited quickly, her photographer's eye feasting on every charming aspect. "This is amazing. I had no idea it would be so lovely here. I don't know where to start."

Clay smiled. "Take your time. We have all afternoon. I'm sure you won't miss a thing."

They started down the sidewalk, and Melody began snapping pictures. She quickly realized there was no way she could capture the charm of every stately home on the block. "Are these the homes of the families who founded Blessing?"

"A few. Most of these mansions belonged to the timber barons and the local merchants who made their fortunes supporting them. The loblolly pine forest here provided Blessing's main industry for decades until oil was discovered."

They reached the first porch, and Melody tensed. It was already crowded with people, and others were approaching from the opposite direction.

"How many porches will we visit?" Her changed appearance still left her feeling awkward. They might not know it was a new look, but she did. What would they think?

"Ten. It's a good turnout. Everyone wants to support the bicentennial. The town has really stepped up."

"Are porch crawls usually this big?"

"It depends. Most of the time, it's only a few neighbors who want to get together. Sometimes it's a small group that wants to promote a club or charity."

Clay lightly touched her elbow as they climbed the broad steps to the generous porch at the light green Queen Anne Victorian. A woman about their age smiled and came to greet them.

"You must be Melody, our book lady," she said. "I'm Jennifer Hill. Welcome to my home. We have refreshments on that end and lively conversation on this end."

Decorated like a Victorian high tea, the Hill porch fairly dripped with Southern elegance. Every detail was perfect, and Melody suspected the utensils and china were all heirlooms. After sampling several of the dainty treats, she listened in on the conversations of the other guests. She found them as fascinated with her task of compiling their town's history as she was to learn about their families' contributions.

She was relieved when Clay came and escorted her to the next porch. This one graced the front of a stately Victorian Eastlake style. The owner, an elderly woman named Miss Ada Lisle, had chosen a floral theme, cramming every inch of the porch with fresh flowers. It was beautiful, but a bit over the top for Melody.

Clay introduced her to the hostess.

"It's nice to meet you, Miss Lisle," she said.

"Ah, you're the book lady. Bless your heart, you had to come all the way down here from up north just to write our little history." She looked Melody up and down before continuing. "I'm sure there are plenty of

Southern girls who could have done a wonderful job and saved you the long trip."

Melody wasn't sure how to take the comment. It sounded kind but something in the way the woman had chosen her words left a big question in her mind. Clay smoothly steered her toward the long table filled with pastries.

"Congratulations. You've passed the first test."

"I have? How?"

"You've survived being insulted by Miss Ada."

She had felt a bit put down. "She wasn't being kind?"

He grinned. "She was complaining that we had to bring a Yankee down here to do a job one of our Southern belles could have done better. That's where the 'bless your heart' comes in."

"That's an insult? It sounded so sweet."

He nodded. "It can be. It can also be a dig at your behavior or your attitude or your choice in colleges. It's a multipurpose insult. It all depends on the tone of voice."

"I think I have a lot to learn about life in a small Southern town."

"No worries. I have your back."

The sincerity in his voice touched her heart. She looked into his eyes and for the first time saw only kindness. "Thank you. That means a lot. I don't want to get on the wrong side of anyone here. I want to write a book that will make them proud of their heritage."

"You will. I have complete confidence in you."

As the day wore on, Melody lost track of names and information and just started inviting everyone to contact her at her annex office. Clay strolled at her side, nodding to those who passed, stopping to talk to others and introducing her. There was no way she could keep up.

By the time they reached the end of the block, Melody was feeling the strain of so much activity. She'd tasted every kind of Southern dessert imaginable, from pecan pie and strawberry tarts to bread pudding and Mississippi mud pie.

Clay rested his hand on the small of her back as they crossed the street to the boulevard park. Ancient live oaks draped with Spanish moss provided shade along the walkway. Melody hesitated, then took a seat on an ornate bench positioned between coral azalea bushes.

Clay took a seat beside her. "Tired?"

"A little, but it's been fun. I've never attended an event like this before."

"Southerners enjoy getting together. We like to talk and eat and sit on our porches watching the world go by."

She smiled, her gaze taking in the colorful surroundings. "I could get used to that kind of life. Slow, peaceful, gentle."

Clay studied her a moment. "Really? I wouldn't have thought that you would. Used to be, you were all about being on the move every moment and looking for excitement."

He wasn't wrong. The old Melody would have been quickly bored with a porch crawl. "I'm older. I've learned to appreciate a less hectic pace of life."

"Hey there, Clay."

A man waved from across the street. Clay waved back. "I need to speak to him. Will you be okay here for a minute?"

"Sure. Go ahead." She watched as he jogged across the street and shared a man-hug with the gentleman. Clay had been kind and thoughtful today. He'd made sure she met everyone and that she tried as many culinary delights as possible. She'd watched him, glad that he seemed to be enjoying the porch crawl, too. He'd laughed and joked with the guests and behaved like the man she remembered.

Their truce was in force, though she sensed an odd undercurrent in him that concerned her. Maybe it was her own insecurities acting up. The Lord knew she was riddled with them.

Her gaze drifted around the park, settling on the tiered fountain at its center. Small planters overflowing with flowers flanked the winding walkway. She'd never appreciated flowers until she'd come to Blessing. Her gaze drifted to Clay, who was still speaking with his friend.

There were a lot of things she'd learned to appreciate since coming to this town. Not the least of which was Clay. As much as she wished it weren't true, her heart still held a deep affection for him.

The beauty of spring displayed in the park seeped into her spirit, filling her with contentment. Every step she took was like walking through a watercolor painting. She looked forward to visiting the homes on the other side of the street and learning more about the town and its history.

She rose and strolled toward the fountain. The trickle of water added a soothing undertone to the birdsong overhead. A faint sound of music floated on the air, and she glanced over to see a young woman cross the street, holding her cell phone and singing softly.

Melody recognized the song and tried to quickly block it from her mind. Too late. The past swooped around her, yanking her back to the office in Shanghai. The song had been playing on her friend's device when the world exploded in noise and smoke and darkness. Her mind replayed the sound of breaking glass. The shouts. The screams. The heat and pain. It was the last thing Melody remembered.

"Melody. Melody!"

Someone touched her shoulder, and she jumped. The scene melted from her internal vision, replaced by the bubbling fountain and colorful blossoms. She became aware of a comforting hand on her arm. She blinked and found Clay standing close at her side. A look of deep concern was etched on his handsome face.

"Are you okay? What's wrong?"

She carefully stepped away, breaking contact. "Nothing. I was…lost in thought." She forced a smile. "Daydreaming. It's the perfect…setting for that, don't you think?" Her voice sounded shaky to her ears. She hoped Clay would ignore it.

"Are you sure? You were in a trance. I had to squeeze your arm to get your attention." His gaze raked her up and down. "You're shaking. Are you ill?"

Melody shook her head. "No. I'm fine." She wasn't going to admit to Clay that she'd had a flashback. He'd want to know why and what had happened. She wasn't going to relive that day for any reason.

She closed her eyes and inhaled slowly. "Really, I'm fine. I guess I was lost in thought. There's so much to learn." She ran out of words so she made a gesture instead, hoping he would let things slide. "I've met a lot of people today."

"Would you like to leave?"

Yes. Desperately, but she'd learned that hiding from

the flashbacks only made them worse. Best to push forward. "No. I want to visit the rest of the porches."

Clay stared at her a little longer, then nodded. "All right. If you're sure you're okay."

"Fit as a fiddle." She started across the street to the sidewalk, trying to put a bounce in her step and praying he wouldn't ask any more questions. The fog in her mind was dissipating and by the time they reached the next house, she was feeling almost normal, though her embarrassment over the flashback still resonated. It was bad enough when they happened in private, but to experience one now, in front of Clay, was too humiliating.

Melody searched for something to say to divert attention from her episode. "So who was your friend?"

"A customer. He's thinking about going with the Delta Company. I think I convinced him to hold off awhile."

"Why are your customers leaving?"

"Delta is offering a much lower price. We won't be able to compete if this keeps up. Add to that the rain we've had over the last few months, and we're unable to spray when the fields are drenched. We're behind, and there's more rain forecast for the next two weeks."

"What are you going to do?"

"I'll think of something. It's not your problem." Clay pointed to the stately Italianate home they were approaching. "You're going to like this family. Their forefathers started the first bank in Blessing."

Melody concentrated on listening to Clay as he explained about the residents and the history of the old home. His quiet voice helped clear her mind and find her center again.

By the time they returned to the car, she was overflowing with information and ideas for the book.

"Thank you for taking me today." She fastened her seat belt and looked over at Clay. "I had a good time. I'm starting to feel like a local."

He looked her way, a grin on his face. "You certainly made an impression on everyone."

What? "Good, I hope."

He laughed. "Of course. You're an easy person to like."

"Wow. A compliment."

"It's the truth. Dad was right. You are the perfect person to write our history."

"Thank you. That means a lot." Their eyes met and just as quickly looked away.

"My issues with you have nothing to do with your job."

"I know. It's personal." She chuckled softly. "Ironic. That's the opposite of what most people say."

Clay pulled up at the cottage and killed the engine. "So what did you think of your first porch crawl?"

"It was wonderful. Fun. When's the next one?"

"Not sure, but the committee is planning at least two more this year. One in the fall and one at Christmas."

"None during the summer?"

He shook his head. "Too hot. You'll understand if you're still here in the summer."

"I should be finished with the book by then. Your dad gave me an end of May deadline." A tiny thread of disappointment surprised her. She hurried on before she could think about it too deeply. "I really did enjoy the day, Clay. Thank you for taking me. Everyone was so friendly and so eager to help. It made me realize that I need to add personal stories to the book. Maybe you can help me decide which ones are most significant."

"I don't know," Clay said slowly. "That would risk making the ones left out mad at me and I have to live here, remember."

It took her a minute to realize he was joking. Like the old days. Then she laughed. "You can blame me. I won't be here to suffer the abuse."

He looked at her oddly, as if he were taking inventory. What was he looking for? The old Melody? He'd be disappointed. She didn't exist anymore. That Melody had died in Shanghai. The person she was now bore no resemblance to that woman. She'd changed from inside out.

She doubted Clay would believe it if she explained it to him.

Chapter Five

Clay parked his vehicle in front of the garage and killed the engine, his thoughts replaying the afternoon with Melody at the porch crawl. She'd been more like the woman he'd fallen in love with—friendly, upbeat and enthusiastic. She'd seemed to be having a wonderful time meeting everyone and trying the local delicacies. But then he'd found her zoned out by the fountain, and he couldn't shake that memory. He'd touched her multiple times and called her name repeatedly before she snapped out of it. His heart had been racing.

Uncle Paul had suffered a PTSD moment once during a family get-together. A loud noise had sent him into a flashback, and he'd huddled in the corner of the room for a long time while his wife talked him back to reality.

Clay rubbed his chin. Dad had wondered if Melody suffered from PTSD, but Clay had dismissed it as nonsense. Now he couldn't ignore the possibility. What had happened to her in the years they'd been apart? He'd envisioned her living the high life, traveling the globe, reporting from world events, her smile lighting up the TV screen each night. It was obvious now, however, that something more disturbing had occurred. What? For all his anger, he'd never wished her any harm. Ever.

His father's comments replayed in his mind as he tried to bring up an image of her from the past. Sadly he couldn't get beyond that look in her eyes the last time he'd seen her. That determined glint in her eyes that he realized now meant goodbye.

Dad had thought she looked pale and frail. Well, she was a Northerner. Give her some time in the sun and her color would improve, wouldn't it? She did seem thinner, but he didn't know a woman who wasn't on some kind of diet. He couldn't remember her ever being concerned about her weight, though.

He growled in frustration. How was he supposed to make a comparison after all this time?

He thought back to the day they'd toured downtown. She'd wanted to know about the businesses and the evolution of the square, but she didn't seem to have the same bounce to her step she'd once had. Of course, neither did he.

Then he thought about her eyes. Their golden-brown color had fascinated him from the beginning. When she was happy, they sparkled like amber, rivaling the brightness of her smile. Now her eyes were a darker shade of brown and the sparkle was gone. She smiled frequently, but he'd noticed it didn't reach her eyes. Why not? What was he seeing? A change in her personality or maturity, or was he just looking to confirm what his dad thought he'd seen?

One thing was certain. She had changed. And he wanted to know how deep that change went.

Eli and Dad had both suggested Melody needed a friend. Maybe it was time he became a real one… And maybe he could start by finding out what she'd been through.

Clay stared at the water in the pond, his mind shuffling through the mounting problems facing Dusty Birds. Rumors were circulating that Delta had offered Clawson Farms a lowball offer for their application services. Clawson was his company's biggest customer. Losing that account could spell disaster for Dusty Birds. Things were bad enough as it was. The Pawnee Brave plane had an engine problem that could cost thousands to fix, and the cost of aviation fuel had gone up.

He cast his line into the water again, wondering whether he should tell his dad about the situation. He'd prefer to handle the problems on his own and keep Dad out of it, but if things got any worse, he'd have to fill him in. He had a right to know.

Leaning back in the yard chair, Clay laid his fishing pole on the ground beside him and stretched out his legs, tilting his face to the sun.

"I don't think you'll catch many fish with your rod in the grass."

Clay recognized the amused voice. Melody. He sat up and looked at her, a warm appreciation filling his veins. She looked fresh and lovely in the morning sunlight. Her shorter hairstyle moved in the breeze. An old memory started to form. He squelched it. "You're up early."

"I'm always up early. I don't sleep well these days."

He started to ask why, but she turned away as if regretting having shared that information. Her canine companion put its paws on his shoe, looking for attention. He reached down and scratched the puppy's ears. "Looks like Barney is a happy guy. How's that working out?"

"Wonderfully. It's nice to have a little friend."

Clay's conscience pricked. He hadn't been much of a friend to Melody since she'd shown up in Blessing. And he'd even thought about that, just a day or two ago. He gestured toward the other yard chair. "Have a seat."

"Thanks." She sat down and smiled at him. "I see you out here every morning. You always look so relaxed and peaceful."

"It's a peaceful place." He wasn't sure how he felt about her watching him.

"So what's wrong this morning? Something is clearly bothering you."

"Why do you say that?"

She smiled. "Because you've done that thumb thing twice since I've been here."

"What thumb thing?"

"You know, the way you drag your thumbnail across your eyebrow when you're worried or stressed."

Clay glanced at his hand. She was right. It was one of his nervous habits. Had she remembered that?

"What's going on, Clay? Can I help? We used to tell each other everything, remember?"

He looked into her eyes. Oh, he remembered. All too well. Still, maybe it would help to run his concerns past an objective person. He broke eye contact when his pulse started to hiccup.

"It's a business thing. I'll work it out."

"What kind of thing?"

He stifled a smile. Once Melody had questions, there was no putting her off. He remembered that, too. He might as well tell her—she'd nag him until he did.

"You remember the man I stepped away to talk to at

the crawl when you were sitting in the park?" She nodded. "He was one of our customers. He's decided since then that he'll be doing business with Delta Ag from now on. They're charging twenty percent less than our company. I can't meet that price."

"I'm sorry."

He inhaled. "It gets worse. Greg Zachary, our part-time pilot, gave notice this morning. He's going to work for Delta. The pay is better. That leaves us shorthanded just as the busy season is gearing up."

"Can you hire another pilot?"

Clay started to rub his eyebrow, then lowered his hand. He didn't like that Melody knew him so well.

"It's not that easy. Ag pilots are highly skilled and in great demand. There's not enough to fill the need."

"Can you train one yourself?"

He smiled. "If only. No. There are only three ag-training schools in the country. The closest one to us is Dallas. Jared and I will have to take up the slack."

"I had no idea crop dusting was so complicated."

"Agricultural application."

She nodded. "Right. Sorry. Does your offer to show me the business still stand? I need to do some research on your family and the company for the history book anyway. Would now be a good time?"

He had a thousand things to do this morning, but the idea of showing off his family business to Melody was more appealing.

"Sure." He stood and picked up his pole and carried it to the porch, hanging it in the rack with the other rods. "We'll take the truck to the airfield. Hop in while I tell Dad where we're going. You might want to leave the dog in the garage while we're gone."

Melody was settled in the passenger seat when he returned. He'd made a quick exit before Dad could bombard him with questions about the book lady and nag him again to tell her the truth about Eli.

Clay slid behind the wheel, noticing Melody had her iPad open on her lap. "Going to document the tour?"

"Of course. It's my job."

Clay drove the short distance to the private airstrip on the property, pulling to a stop near the three yellow planes painted with the Dusty Birds logo. He really should be firing up the Ag Cat and heading to Fisher's farm, but he'd rather show Melody around. He needed to do it sooner rather than later anyway.

Melody strolled toward the planes lined up perfectly near the small metal hangar. "They're beautiful. But I was expecting them to look like biplanes, with the wings on top."

"That's old-school. Planes today have the wings on the bottom of the fuselage with the spray bars mounted below that."

"Why are they all different?"

"Different planes for different applications. The Pawnee Brave, the one with the blue stripe, is the oldest. It's going to need a new engine soon. The Thrush Commander with the green stripe is a two-seater. It has a top speed of one hundred and twenty-two knots and, fully loaded, can carry a total capacity of six thousand pounds of product."

He walked to the last plane in the row. "But the Air Tractor is our workhorse. With a payload of over nine thousand pounds and an eight-hundred-gallon hopper, this baby is the best. With its power, speed and payload, we can stay longer over the field and complete more jobs in a single load."

He glanced at Melody and found her smiling, her brown eyes twinkling. "What?"

"You really love your work, don't you? I can hear the enthusiasm in your voice and see the joy on your face."

His cheeks warmed and he looked away. "Yeah, I guess I do."

"I'm glad to see you happy. You deserve to be."

A lump lodged in his throat. He didn't deserve to be happy, not as long as he was harboring his cruel secret. He met her gaze. "You deserve to be happy, too, Melody. Are you?" He could see his comment caught her off guard.

"Yes, I suppose. As happy as I can be. I love my job, I'm enjoying being here in Blessing and—" she took a breath "—I'm enjoying seeing you again."

Their eyes locked, and he swallowed hard. He wanted to admit that he was glad to see her again, but the words stuck in his throat. Melody looked away first, clearly uncomfortable with the conversation.

She pointed to the other side of the hangar. "What's that one over there?"

"My private plane. A Cessna. It's for pleasure more than work."

"Do you fly it often?"

"Whenever I have the time. I'm teaching Eli to fly."

Her eyes widened. "Really? Maybe you could teach me, too. I've always wanted to learn to fly."

He swallowed again against the lump in his throat. The idea of him and Melody close together in the small cockpit was far too appealing. "I'm not sure you'll be here long enough."

She blushed and turned back to the row of planes. "Can I see inside one?"

"Sure." He held out his hand to help her up onto the

wing, then opened the door, forgetting how close she would have to stand to see the cockpit. He breathed in a citrus scent mingled with the fresh air of morning. "You can sit in the seat if you want."

"Oh, no. I'd be afraid I'd mess something up. This looks like the controls to a spaceship."

Clay chuckled, relieved to be on comfortable footing again. "It's not that bad, but there's a lot to keep your eyes on."

"Is that a computer?"

Clay did a quick explanation of the dials and gauges and how the computerized information helped him start and stop the spray. Melody hung on his every word. That surprised him. He'd expected her to pay polite attention, then be eager to leave.

"This is amazing." She met his gaze. "I always knew you were smart, but I never realized how skilled you are. I also never expected crop dusting uh, agricultural application—to be so specialized."

"It is these days."

She fell silent a long moment. "This is a dangerous job, isn't it?"

Her question touched him. "It can be. You have to be aware every minute. There's a lot to keep track of. You have to know when to start and stop the application to prevent overspray on homes and other crops. You don't want pesticide to drift over onto a field that needs fungicide. That could be disastrous for the farmer."

Melody studied him, then looked back to the cockpit. "I can see why you would need a computer."

He nodded. "Wind plays a big factor, as well. If it changes even a degree, it can force you to recalibrate everything."

Clay jumped down from the wing and reached up to help Melody down. She rested her hands on his shoulders as he lowered her to the ground. He was surprised at how light she was and how thin. A stiff breeze could blow her away. He started to ask her about her health, then thought better of it. No need to rock the boat.

"Thank you, Clay. I have a whole new respect for what you do. I may have more questions later, if that's all right."

"Anytime." He looked into her golden-brown eyes and forgot to breathe. Memories of their times together rushed through his mind with torrential force, bringing an awareness that he didn't want to acknowledge. He searched for something to say to break the awkward moment.

"Um, so how's the book coming?"

"Good. I've started writing the first chapter. I'd like you to take a look at it when you have time."

"Not sure I'd be a good judge. My job was to help you gather information, not edit the content." He started back to the truck.

"I know. But you're a resident of Blessing, and I'd like to know how the opening seems to you. Does it sound stuffy, interesting or just plain dull?"

"I doubt anything you do would be dull." Heat rushed into his cheeks, and he turned away. What had come over him?

"That's kind of you. I'd better get back. I have an appointment with Keisha Monroe. She's been collecting the African American history of Blessing for years. It'll be invaluable to the book. I don't want to be late meeting her."

"Okay. I'll drop you at the garage so you can pick up Barney."

They rode in silence back to the house. Melody opened the door the moment he stopped the truck. She smiled, thanked him again, then hurried off. He wondered briefly if she was hurrying because of her appointment or because she wanted away from him.

He hoped it was the former.

Rain was falling steadily, as it had for the last two days. Perfect weather for writing. She'd written rough drafts of chapters two and three and organized information for the next. This afternoon she planned to tackle the photos. There were so many wonderful images, it would be difficult to cull them down to the ones she could use in the book. She needed an assistant who could copy all the photos and keep them organized so she could return them to their owners when she was finished. Eli would be the perfect choice. He was such a sweet young boy. She hadn't spent much time around children. Never thought she had anything in common with them, but from the moment she met Eli she'd felt an affinity, probably because he was Clay's son. The Reynolds charm was hard to resist.

Barney barked and ran to the front door. Melody glanced out the window and saw Eli. She pulled the door open with a smile. "I was just thinking about you. Come in."

Eli pulled off his poncho and boots and left them on the porch. "I finished my homework, and Dad said I could come visit. I wish he'd let me help you, but he says he's still thinking about it."

Melody took a seat on the sofa and motioned Eli to have a seat. "I'll talk to him again and see if I can convince him."

"What would I do? Would I get to use the cameras?"

"Definitely. I need help with all the photos I have. A lot of them are in books or belong to the people who live here. Since I can't keep them, I need to make copies."

"Like on a copy machine? I've used the one at the hangar."

"That's good to know, but I'm taking photos with my camera. It makes an image that can be uploaded to my computer. I was hoping you'd take charge of that for me."

Eli smiled. "That'd be so cool." Barney put his paws on Eli's shins, wagging his tail.

Eli reached down and petted him. "He's getting big. We gave the last of the litter to Mr. Cooper today. I wanted to keep one of the pups for myself, but Dad said no. He thinks Lady is enough."

Melody smiled. "Well, Barney will be here for you to play with. In fact, I could use someone who knows about dogs. I have no clue. Maybe, when I go home, I could leave Barney with you. If it's okay with your dad."

"You won't take him with you?"

"I doubt it. I don't know where I'll be after the book is finished." The realization of that fact left a dull ache in her chest.

"You could stay here."

"I'd like that, but I'd have to find a job."

"We have jobs here," Eli pointed out.

Melody smiled and touched his shoulder, resisting the urge to hug him. "Why don't I show you what you'd be doing if your dad agrees?"

Eli nodded and followed her to the office she'd set up in the second bedroom. She was in the process of showing him how to tag the photos when her cell rang. Clay's name was displayed. She answered, glancing at Eli as his dad asked her to send him home.

"Time to go home, Eli."

He rolled his eyes. "That was my dad, huh?"

She nodded. "Afraid so. But I'll talk to him again soon, so keep your fingers crossed."

Out on the porch, Melody saw the rain had stopped. "I think I'll sit out here awhile. I'm really grateful for this porch."

Eli frowned. "But you don't have a chair out here."

She smiled. "I'm going to get a rocker as soon as I have a free moment. In the meantime, I just use a kitchen chair."

They waved goodbye, and she watched him run through the puddles as he hurried home. She enjoyed his company. She hoped Clay would relent and let his son help her out.

There was something special about the boy. She couldn't explain it, but she was drawn to him. Maybe she was simply feeling her age and realizing she'd never have a child of her own.

Melody stepped into the Reynoldses' small library and smiled. Every wall was covered with books. Dave had given her permission to look through them all, and she was eager to get started. Over the last few weeks, she'd gained a solid overall picture of Blessing's history and had outlined a possible sequence for the book. Now it was down to the details and balancing which events were to be included. The Reynolds family was one of the last founding families for her to research.

She also had yet to meet with the owner of the old plantation. She'd been warned that the reclusive man wasn't likely to agree to a meeting and her best bet would be to meet with his assistant or local historian Jeffrey Hollis, who knew more about the original owners than anyone else.

She set up her laptop, then started perusing the rows of books. The family history was conveniently arranged right near the desk. She pulled out two and settled in. Two hours later she stretched and rubbed her eyes. The Reynolds family background was going to take up more space than she'd first thought. Clay came from a long line of hardworking, civic-minded people. They'd been merchants and farmers when Blessing was a fledgling community. Later they'd become successful in the logging industry before going into politics. Two former mayors were Reynolds men before Dave took office. The crop-dusting business had grown steadily and provided a good living for the family.

Clay's concerns about Dusty Birds came to mind. She'd prayed that the loss of his part-time pilot wouldn't put the company in trouble. She didn't like the thought of Clay stressed over his family business. She wished there were something she could do.

"How's it going, Miss Melody?"

Melody smiled as Dave entered the library. "Good afternoon. It's going great. I'm learning so much about your family. They made a huge contribution to Blessing. You must be very proud."

"I am. But I'm more proud of my son and grandson."

Melody smiled. "Of course. And you should be. They're special people."

"Clay is a good man. I'd like him to find a good woman someday."

She wasn't sure how to respond to that. Was Dave fishing for her opinion of Clay, or did he have match-making on his mind? What would he say if she told him she and Clay had a past?

"I'm sure he will."

"I hope." He grinned and tugged on his ear. "It won't be easy to find the right woman. She'd have to be smart, loving, strong and devoted. Not an easy combination to find these days. Most women are focused on their careers, not family."

Melody dropped her gaze to the computer screen. He was talking about her, the old her. Her heart clenched. What should she say? "Sometimes people have to work at their careers before they discover that other things are more important."

"I suppose you're right." He slipped his hands into his pockets. "I won't keep you. I mainly stopped by to invite you to dinner tonight. We're having a family favorite. Chicken and noodles."

"Oh, that's very nice of you but I wouldn't want to intrude."

"Nonsense. You're practically family. You live next door, and you claimed one of our puppies."

His invitation was too sweet to turn down. Hopefully the truce between her and Clay would hold. "I'd love to come. Can I bring anything?"

"Just yourself and a healthy appetite."

"I'm looking forward to it." It wasn't a total lie, but she had to admit to some trepidation at the thought of being part of their family meal. Watching the Reynolds men had opened a new perspective for her. The family closeness left a small kernel of sadness in her heart and a growing sense of envy. What would her life have been like if she'd chosen a different path? What if she'd kept her child instead of chasing after a dream that had evaporated in the chill of reality?

Chapter Six

Clay maneuvered the controls of the Air Tractor, setting it down on the runway with a slight bounce. He taxied the plane into its normal parking position, then shut down the controls. With a sigh, he removed his headset and closed his eyes. He'd nearly crashed today. The tree line at the end of the field had loomed before him, and it was all he could do to lift the plane above it. The Lord had been watching out for him today.

He ran a hand through his hair. It was his own fault. He'd lost focus and allowed his mind to wander to Melody. Normally, he prided himself on his ability to concentrate on all the dozens of details he needed to be aware of when he was in the air. He couldn't afford to misjudge the wind speed or forget to keep an eye on the terrain.

Having Melody back in his life was playing havoc with his mental state. Eli kept bugging him to go see her. He was fascinated with her cameras. He'd even sneaked over there once, but she hadn't been home.

If that wasn't bad enough, rumors were flying about the Delta Company and how they were approaching ag pilots and businesses and luring employees away. Sooner or later, he'd have to tell Dad, if he hadn't heard the gossip already.

Climbing out of the cockpit, he secured the plane and entered the hangar. Half an hour later, he closed up and headed to the house. He was looking forward to his dad's chicken and noodles tonight. It had been his favorite meal since he was a kid.

The moment he stepped inside the kitchen, he knew something was up. There was an impish grin on Dad's face that always, *always* spelled trouble. For Clay.

He walked to the stove, bracing himself. "What's going on?"

Dad shrugged. "Nothing much. How'd your day go?"

Clay wasn't about to tell him about his near crash. Besides, his dad didn't really care about his day. He was focused on whatever idea had popped up in his head. "Fine. Pretty routine. I'm looking forward to a big plate of noodles."

"Good. But you'll have to be on your best behavior tonight. We're having company."

"Oh?" Clay prepared to hear the name of a friend or one of Dad's buddies. "Who's coming to dinner?"

"Melody." He grinned like a Cheshire cat.

Clay wasn't sure he'd heard right. "Melody. Why?"

"Because she's nice and Eli likes her. I like her. She's working hard on this book." He set the kitchen spoon aside and faced him. "She worked for hours today in your grandpa's library. I thought she could use a home-cooked meal."

There wasn't much Clay could say. He couldn't disagree with a single thing his dad had said. But having

Melody at the same table with Eli, sharing a meal, was more family togetherness than he'd bargained for.

From out of nowhere, a surge of longing invaded his mind. The three of them were a family. But adding Melody to the mix created a different picture. They would be a complete family. Mother, father, child, grandparent. The thought should have sent shock waves through his system. Instead he found himself wishing they really were a real and honest family. He tried not to think about what Eli was missing in not having a mother. He'd always told himself it wasn't important and that he and his dad were enough.

But was it?

"You okay with this, son? I hope so—she'll be here any moment."

What could he say? *I hate it. Don't let her in?* "Sure, Dad. It'll be nice. And you're right. She has worked hard and deserves one of your great home-cooked meals."

Clay went to clean up, reminding himself it was only supper. A meal with a friend.

If only he could forget that it was a meal with Eli's mother.

Melody settled in the dining room, watching as Clay and Eli brought the food to the table. She'd offered to help but they'd refused. She'd kept her gaze on Clay to see if he was unhappy with her joining them, but he appeared relaxed. That eased much of her anxiety. She liked seeing him in this domestic setting. It suited him. The playful banter between the Reynolds men made her smile.

With everything on the table, they took their seats and joined hands. As Dave said grace, Melody held Clay's hand and fought off memories of holding hands and walking through the park and along Tybee Beach. With determination, she shut down those images and let the conversation drift around her as she ate the tasty meal.

A brief sense of contentment settled over her shoulders, but it was quickly replaced with a deep sense of loss. Her throat seized up, making it hard to swallow. Tears stung the backs of her eyes and she fought them down. She'd never known a pleasant family dinner growing up. Most of the foster homes she'd lived in were chaotic and dysfunctional. Mama Kay's home was the first place she'd experienced a real family atmosphere. Mama's husband, Mark, had said grace each night and read the Bible out loud in the evenings. He'd helped with homework and teased her about boys and her love of chocolate. She wondered if Eli knew how fortunate he was having a father and a grandfather.

As she watched the family interact, an old faded dream began to reform. She couldn't change the past, but maybe someday she could have a family of her own. A child of her own. Shame and regret washed through her veins. She'd had a son. She'd given him up with hardly a thought. She'd sought the Lord's forgiveness for her past actions and choices, but the memory still had the power to sting like fire through her veins whenever it surfaced.

Forcing aside her gloomy thoughts, she concentrated on Eli, who was telling a story about his friends at school. Eli was a sweet boy, bright, inquisitive and polite.

Eli, who was not much younger than her own son would be, wherever he was.

Enough of that! She set her fork down and said the first thing that came to her head.

"Clay, have you thought any more about Eli coming over to help me with the book?"

Clay froze, gripping his fork tightly. She closed her eyes, already regretting her words. She should have spoken to him privately.

"Can I, Dad? Please. I'll get my homework done, I promise. I want to help. She already showed me what I'd have to do and it's easy. And I get to use her cool camera."

Melody shot a glance at Clay, relieved to see there was no steam coming from his ears. "He is a quick learner and I could use the help. But only if it's all right with you."

The muscle in Clay's jaw flexed briefly. "I guess it would be all right. But your school and chores come first."

"Woo-hoo! When can I start?"

Melody laughed at his enthusiasm. "Come over tomorrow after school and I'll get you started."

"Awesome. Thanks, Dad."

The look on Clay's face now was pinched, as if he already regretted his decision. Wanting to keep busy, Melody helped clear the table. Alone with Clay, she thought it might be a good idea to offer an apology.

"I'm sorry for speaking up about Eli helping me. I should have talked to you alone. I really would enjoy having him around and he would be a big help."

"He's ten. What can he do?"

"A lot. Taking pictures, for one thing. I can't take apart all these family histories, so I take pictures of pages and documents to go over later. Eli could easily do that and save me a lot of time. It might make him feel like he was part of the project, too."

"Maybe."

Clearly, he had more thinking to do. Best she leave him alone for now. "I'd better go. Thank you for inviting me. Everything was delicious. I can't remember a more enjoyable meal." Her voice caught on the words and she turned away, unwilling to let Clay see her raw emotions. She had enjoyed the evening more than she'd ever expected and didn't want it to end.

"Is something wrong? Are you all right?"

She nodded, collecting herself before facing him and forcing a smile. "Everything was perfect. I haven't had many family suppers in my life. It makes me wish I had a real family."

"Maybe you will someday."

"No. Not now. Not after all I've done." She raised her chin. "I'd better run. I'm expecting a call from Mrs. Van Buren. Tell your dad and Eli goodbye for me."

"Melody, wait."

"Talk to you later."

She hurried outside and across the lawn toward the cottage. Joy and sadness, regret and gratitude all battled in her mind as she walked. The evening had been perfect. If she'd chosen differently, she could have had a home and family. *This* family, even. But she'd been too young and too ignorant to understand what she was sacrificing.

Inside the cottage, she scooped up Barney, turned out the lights and went to her bedroom. Fatigue pulled her down. It had been a long day, but she'd made great strides. Two recent interviews with locals had given her new and interesting information for the book, and Deborah had dropped off a jump drive containing old newspaper articles from 1900 to 1940. Melody couldn't wait to dig into them.

Unbuttoning her shirt, she glanced at herself in the mirror. Slowly, she removed her blouse. Her gaze automatically landed on her left arm and the scarred tissue running from her shoulder to right above her wrist. Just looking at it brought a lump to her throat. After two years, the puckered and whitened skin still had the power to trigger depression. She touched the scar lightly, closing her eyes to the ugly sight.

Then she deliberately shifted her thoughts to gratitude, uttering a soft prayer for forgiveness. As much as the bombing had taken from her, the Lord had given back threefold.

The surgeries, the long rehabilitation, the emotional trenches she'd had to climb out of—they'd stripped away her old ideas and assumptions about life. The Lord had set her on a new path, filled with hope. God's mercy had restored her. If an ugly scarred arm was the price she had to pay, it was worth it. Ten times over. She'd emerged from that horrible event stronger, saner and with a contentment she'd never known before. She was still subject to brief bouts of depression and insecurity, but they were fewer now.

Opening the tube of ointment, she applied it lightly to the scars to keep the skin supple. What would Clay think if he saw her arm? Would he pity her? Would he believe she deserved what she got after the way she'd left? No. Clay would never wish harm on anyone. His attitude toward her was understandable. Thankfully, he was easing up on that.

Maybe someday they could come out the other side as friends. It was the most she could ask for.

Clay stood on the front porch watching Melody hurry back to the cottage. He'd been caught off guard by her reaction to supper. Sometimes he forgot that she'd been raised in foster care, devoid of the warmth of family that had surrounded him all his life. One of the things he'd always admired about her was her strength and determination to overcome her difficult past.

He'd have to be more sensitive to her history from here on. He had no desire to cause her pain. He'd enjoyed the evening meal, too. She'd appeared relaxed and happy. It wasn't until she'd brought up the subject of Eli helping her that he'd had a problem.

Every impulse in his body still shouted no, but Dad's warning was never far from his mind. If he made too much of them spending time together, it could backfire. He was stuck between the infamous rock and a hard place.

Clay remained on the porch until the lights went out in the cottage, then he took a seat on the swing. He needed a few minutes to himself to think things through. His secrets were eating away at him. Not only did he carry the truth about Melody and Eli on his shoulders, but he was also keeping the business problems from his father. And he was tired.

Dusty Birds had been hit hard financially last year and this year wasn't looking any better. It had been the wettest spring and summer on record. You couldn't spray when it was raining. The downtime was cutting deep into their operating budget and the forecast for the summer was more of the same. If this kept up, Dusty Birds would be out of business. He couldn't let that happen. His family had kept the business running for generations. It wasn't going to die on his watch. He was doing his best to shield Dad from the truth of the situation, but if things got worse they'd have to face facts. Dad would be heartbroken. He was so proud of the company.

Clay entered the kitchen to find his dad mixing up a batch of brownies. "How can you be hungry after that huge meal?"

Dave chuckled. "This has nothing to do with hunger. I had a hankering for chocolate, and Eli made a special request."

"Ah. I should have guessed." Eli had his grandpa wrapped up like a prized turkey.

"Did you enjoy the meal? Melody was a nice addition, don't you think?"

Clay knew his dad was fishing for a positive comment, hoping he was changing his attitude toward Melody. "If you say so."

"Eli enjoyed her being here. He told me it was like having a whole family."

"He said that?"

"He did. He said it was nice and he sometimes wished he had a mom to have dinner with."

"I know what you're trying to do, Dad, but it won't work. I'm not going to tell him about Melody."

"Not ever?"

Clay rubbed his chin. "Eventually."

Dave poured the batter into a rectangular pan. "Unless he discovers the truth himself."

"Not going to happen."

Dad shrugged. "Don't be so sure."

"Are you going to tell him?" Surely he wouldn't stoop so low.

"Me? Of course not. But I think there's an invisible bond between mother and child, and it might rear its head in ways you don't expect."

"I've got this under control, Dad. Don't worry. And I'll tell Eli when the time is right."

His dad smiled sadly. "I'm not sure that's up to you. Oh, by the way, do you know anything about Southern Ag Air closing down?"

Clay had heard the rumor. In fact, he'd planned to call the owner, Carl Edison, in the morning. "It's probably speculation. Carl would never shut down."

"I don't know. That company that bought out Sam Jenkins's business—what's their name, Delta something? I've heard they're buying up a lot of the smaller crop-dusting companies."

"Delta Agricultural Applications."

"That's it. Jenkins should never have sold out to them. But he told me he had no choice. He couldn't compete."

Clay's conscience stung. Should he tell his dad the state of their affairs? "Maybe he didn't. Last year was tough on all of us. With all this rain, this year isn't looking good."

Dave shook his head. "I know, but those big outfits tend to gobble up small businesses one day and go belly up a few months later. This Delta thing is like a corporate raider of crop dusting. Promise me you won't let them come after us."

"Don't worry, Dad. I won't let anything happen to the company." He patted his dad's shoulder reassuringly, but inside his burden grew. How could he admit he might not be able to keep that promise?

Melody stared out the window of her small annex office and sighed. The steady rain that had been falling over the last three days had finally eased up to a light mist. As much as she enjoyed rainy days for writing, the dreary weather had begun to wear on her. The forecast called for sunshine this afternoon and she looked forward to taking Barney for a walk. He needed more exercise than simply tossing a ball across the living room.

"Miss Williams."

Melody looked up at the woman who stood in her doorway. "Yes. Come in. Can I help you?"

The woman smiled, her blue eyes filled with a friendly light. "I hope I can help you."

Melody motioned her to be seated. "Sorry for the cramped quarters. I normally work at home, but this is a good location to meet with people from town."

"My name is Julia Temple. My husband and I bought the Dickson Home on Olive Street. It's in the historic district, and we've been doing extensive remodeling."

"Sounds like a big job."

"More than we anticipated, I'm afraid. We recently opened up a walled-off section of the attic and found several boxes filled with old newspapers, journals and a few letters. I thought they might be helpful in researching the bicentennial history book."

Melody's heart raced. "They would indeed. I can only learn so much from books and looking at family photos. Newspapers would be a wonderful source of information."

"I have the boxes in my car. Should I bring them in?"

"No. Let's put them in my car. I'm leaving shortly. I'll go through them this evening where I can spread them out."

Melody followed Mrs. Temple outside and transferred the old misshapen cardboard boxes to her trunk. Her mind was whirling with excitement, anticipating the stories she might uncover.

"I can't thank you enough for this," she said. "I'm sure these will prove to be a valuable addition to the book. I'll take good care of them and return them as soon as possible."

Mrs. Temple shook her head. "No need. I don't want them back. Feel free to donate them to the library or a local historical organization. We were told when we bought the home that one of its earlier owners, a Walter Merritt, was the editor of the local paper, the *Dispatch*."

"It's now called the *Banner*. I've run across that during my research. Merritt went on to own the paper, then his heirs sold out in the fifties and it became the *Banner*." Melody extended her hand. "Thank you so much."

"You are most welcome. I'll let you know if we find anything else. There's still an entire section of the attic that we haven't opened up yet."

"I'll keep my fingers crossed."

It was all Melody could do to keep from skipping back inside the annex. What a fantastic find. Real newspapers from the 1900s, not microfiche or copies on a jump drive. She couldn't wait to dig into the contents of those boxes. It would be like opening an early Christmas gift.

Clay settled his son in the armchair and gently lifted his bandaged ankle onto the ottoman.

Eli winced. "It hurts."

"I know. I'll get your medication. That'll take the edge off. Be glad it's not broken."

Eli looked up at him with a pleading gaze. "I'll miss the tournament this weekend."

"But you should be better for the next one in Biloxi. If you do everything the doctor tells you."

"I know. I will."

Clay stroked Eli's hair, his heart bursting with gratitude that his son hadn't sustained a more serious injury. "Are you hungry? I'll fix you a sandwich."

The quiet of the kitchen afforded Clay a moment to release his tension. What had started out as normal Little League baseball game had ended in a trip to the emergency room. He'd existed in a state of fear from the moment he realized Eli was hurt. His imagination had taken over, envisioning the worst possible outcomes.

Someone tapped on the back door, and he looked over his shoulder to find Melody looking through the glass. He motioned her in. She hurried toward him, clearly upset.

"Is his leg broken? How is he?"

Clay held up a hand. "It's not broken. It's only a bad ankle sprain. He'll be good as new in a week or so. How did you hear about it?"

"Sandy called me. Her neighbor's son plays on the team." She took a deep breath and shrugged. "I guess the news got distorted along the way. May I see him?"

He had a moment of hesitation. Was her concern because she liked Eli or was it something deeper, a sense that Eli was more than just the landlord's son? Finally, he relented.

"He's in the living room."

Clay fixed a peanut butter and banana sandwich and a drink for Eli and took it to him with his medications. Melody was seated beside him talking softly. She smiled as he entered.

"I'm so thankful it wasn't more serious."

"Me, too."

She peered at the sandwich. "Is that a peanut butter and banana sandwich?"

Eli nodded. "My favorite."

Melody's face lit with a big smile. "Me, too. How about that. You, me and Elvis."

"Who?"

"Oh, my. Now I feel old."

Eli ate a few bites, then said he was tired. The medication was kicking in. Clay handed him the crutches and helped him down the hall to his room. When he returned, Melody was staring out the window. She turned when she heard him, and he saw tears in her eyes.

"Are you all right?"

She nodded. "I was so scared. I thought he'd broken his leg. The rumors were bad. I couldn't stand the thought of him being hurt. What happened?"

His chest filled with pride. "When he slid into home plate, he got tangled up with the catcher and twisted his ankle."

"Poor baby."

Clay dragged his thumb across his eyebrow. Should he tell her now? She was obviously deeply affected by the injury. Would it ease her mind if she knew Eli was her son or only add more sorrow? *No.* Instead, he just muttered, "He'll be fine."

"Is there anything I can do to help?"

The truth was he did need help. He'd explore a few more options before he took that route, though. "No. Though I'm sure he would enjoy your company."

She sighed. "He'll be in good hands with you and your dad."

"Dad isn't here. He left yesterday for Ravenport, North Carolina. He's meeting with their city officials about their bicentennial celebration last year. He won't be home for a week to ten days."

"Who will take care of Eli while you're working?"

"I don't know yet. The weather has finally cleared up and I'll be in the air from dawn to dusk."

"I'll take care of him. He can stay with me while you're working."

"No." He'd responded too quickly. He could see the hurt in her eyes. "You have work to do."

"It's only for a short while. He's already started helping me after school. Plus, it'll keep him occupied and off his feet while he recovers."

"I don't think that's such a good idea."

"Why not? I can get his assignments from school so he doesn't fall behind in his studies. There's only a few weeks left before school lets out. I can even take him to his doctor's appointments. Then you'll be free to concentrate on your work. You said you were behind. This would give you a chance to catch up."

"I'll think about it. Later."

Clay was relieved when Melody finally left. Her offer made sense. It was a practical solution to his dilemma. Only it would place Eli totally under her care and risk his secret being exposed. Maybe he should deal with this now and face the consequences. He sighed. Again, no. It might be the right thing to do, but he wasn't ready. He wasn't sure he ever would be.

Like it or not, judgment day was right around the corner.

Melody walked into her workroom, smiling when she saw Eli working away at the desk. He'd proved to be a real blessing with the book project. He was eager, diligent and competent. At ten years of age, he wasn't as easily distracted by the historical images as she was. Her curiosity always drew her off in other directions, wondering about the family and what happened to them down the years.

Her time with Eli was over tomorrow. His ankle was completely healed. She'd thoroughly enjoyed taking care of him this week. She'd been his tutor and his guardian. She'd gotten his assignments from his teachers and taken him to checkups with the doctor. It was almost like being his mother.

How she would have loved that. Coming to Blessing had been like opening a window to all she'd missed. Her younger self had traded away a life of love and happiness for a promise of success and notoriety. Things she'd once foolishly thought would bring her peace.

It had taken an explosion and a trip to Blessing to show her what really mattered. A sad smile lifted her lips as she watched Eli hard at work. He might not be her son, but for one lovely week she had pretended that he was.

Walking up behind him, Melody placed a hand on his shoulder. He glanced up and smiled.

"You're a big help, Mr. Eli. I'm so glad your dad let you work with me."

"Me, too. I'm going to be a photographer when I grow up. But I want to take pictures of nature. Like dogs and horses and wild animals." He swiveled in the chair, his eyes bright. "Oh, and I think it would be cool to take pictures from the air, too. I could be a pilot like Dad, only I'd fly over the mountains and take pictures of things from up high."

Melody's heart swelled with pride. Her affection and admiration for Clay and his son grew every day.

"That's a wonderful idea. In fact, I think some aerial shots of Blessing would be a good addition to the book. Not only an overview of the history on the ground, but a view from above of the whole town." She leaned over and kissed Eli on the cheek. "You are a brilliant boy, Eli. I don't know what I would do without you."

Eli blushed and lowered his head. "I wish you didn't have to leave Blessing."

"Me, too, but we can still stay in touch through email or Twitter, and we can FaceTime."

"I know, but it's not the same. I didn't know my mom. I don't even have a picture of her. Dad says there aren't any."

"I don't have any pictures of my mom either."

Eli looked at her with sad blue eyes. "Did she die when you were a baby?"

"No. I was about your age when she passed away, but I hadn't seen her for years. She wasn't a very good mother. She left me and my…me alone a lot. I was put in foster care when I was nine."

"Does that mean you had lots of different families? My friend Toby is in foster care. Sometimes the other kids make fun of him."

Melody nodded. "That happened to me, too, sometimes. And yes, I lived with many families, but eventually I ended up with a genuinely nice couple who treated me like one of their own. There were two of us who lived there. Miss Sandy, your Sunday school teacher, was the other one. We became like sisters. We're still close. She helped me get this job."

Eli stared at the desk a moment. "Dad won't talk

about my mom. Every time I ask questions, he says it's not important."

Melody's heart warmed. Poor boy. "It's important to you, though, isn't it?"

Eli nodded.

Melody knew she was treading a fine line with this subject. She wanted to confront Clay and explain to him how important it was to tell his son about his mom.

She wished she had more information about her own mother. Why had she been an alcoholic? What had happened in her life to drive her to drink, and what demons had plagued her and made her leave her two children alone for hours, sometimes days on end? Knowing why might have helped her understand and maybe even figure out her own behavior.

She turned toward the door. "Would you like a snack? How about some popcorn?"

Eli nodded. "Can we have chocolate on it?"

Melody stopped and stared. "You like that, too? I love chocolate on my popcorn."

Eli giggled. "Dad and Gramps think it's weird."

"I hear ya. My sister said I was dumb. She tried it once but hated it."

"They don't know what they're missing."

Melody held up her hand and Eli gave her a high five. "Let's go make some popcorn."

"Yeah! We don't care what those people think. We love it."

Melody wrapped her arm around Eli's shoulder and they made their way to the kitchen. This had been the best day she'd had in a long time. Maybe the best ever.

Chapter Seven

The weather had held for the last week, allowing Clay and Jared to get caught up on their customers. They had a short break now before the next round of applications were scheduled. Clay knew he couldn't have done it without Melody's help. As much as he had worried about leaving his son in Melody's care, the arrangement had worked out well. Eli had enjoyed his time with her and taking photos so much that he'd even requested a camera for his birthday.

He needed to do something to show Melody his appreciation. Lunch at an outdoor café along the river walk should be appropriate. Or should he do more? Buy her a gift? Give her a bonus? Neither idea felt right. A gift might send the wrong message, and a bonus would reduce her kindness in taking care of Eli to a job. He grinned as he imagined her reaction. She'd be furious, hurt and likely to give him a black eye. For all the changes he'd seen in her since coming to Blessing, her fierce determination hadn't diminished in the slightest.

But lunch—he could do that. All he had to do was get up the courage to ask her. She wasn't at the cottage, so he drove into town and checked her annex office. He found her huddled over the small desk between piles of papers. Her hands were supporting her chin, and she looked dejected.

"It can't be all that bad, can it?" She glanced up, her eyes red and puffy as if she'd been crying. "What's wrong?"

She wiped her eyes. "Nothing. Just a bout of self-pity. It'll pass."

He decided against asking her more. "Well, then I might have the perfect antidote. I'd like to treat you to lunch at the River View Café. A thank-you for your help with Eli while I've been working."

She leaned back in her chair and smiled. "That sounds wonderful."

Within minutes, they were seated at an outside table near the ornate cast-iron fence that separated the café patio from the sidewalk. Clay watched her as they waited for their order. She already looked more relaxed. The pinched line around her lips had softened, and her eyes had regained much of their usual sparkle. She exhaled a soft sigh and smiled at him, causing a small blip in his heartbeat.

"This was a wonderful idea. Thank you. I usually grab a sandwich at lunch and keep working." Her gaze shifted to the grassy park on the other side of the river where residents were enjoying the outdoors. "The park is the perfect place for families to come and enjoy each other. Your dad did a wonderful thing here."

It hit him that she probably had few, if any, memories of happy family times.

"It is a popular spot," he agreed. "We could bring a picnic out here one weekend if you'd like." Too late, he realized how she might interpret that invitation. "With Dad and Eli, of course."

Her eyebrows lifted slightly. "Of course."

Warmth crawled up his nerves. He might as well have stated he didn't want to be with her. Thankfully, their food arrived, saving him from further embarrassment.

Melody kept the conversation light as they ate, sharing amusing stories of Eli during his stay with her. By the time dessert arrived, Clay was feeling encouraged. He wanted to ask her what had happened after she walked out ten years ago, but he didn't want to risk getting into the truth. Nor did he want to give anything away.

Again, he searched for a way to begin but lost his courage. Especially sitting across the table from her. Maybe a stroll down the river walk would make things easier. She agreed with a warm smile that sent a jolt of awareness through him. Her smile had always left him weak in the knees. It was the most beautiful sight he'd ever seen. It still was, only now the brilliance of her smile had a softer, muted patina. Its power, however, hadn't diminished.

He gathered his courage and opened his mouth to speak, but Melody spoke first.

"I want to apologize for the way things ended between us." She pulled a leaf from the shrub as they passed. "I shouldn't have left without talking to you. I should have given you an answer at least."

"Why didn't you?"

"I panicked. I saw my plans falling apart, all my dreams melting away. I decided to run instead of staying and working things out."

"Facing the music."

"In a way."

"What happened to you after you left?" He kept his gaze straight ahead, unwilling to see her expression.

"I went back home to my foster mom in Des Moines."

"I looked for you. I thought you might go there but I didn't know her name." It had cost him a sizable sum to hire a detective to track her down.

"Yeah… I've realized that we didn't learn much about each other during that time. We were too busy having fun. It was like a surprise birthday party every time we were together."

"A party. I thought it was more than that." He'd been so certain they'd been on the same wavelength about their feelings. His first mistake.

"I think we should have talked about more serious things."

Clay set his jaw. "Like a future? Or maybe the news you gave me that night about our baby." The words came out hard and accusing. He'd better adjust his tone or she'd be gone again.

Melody stiffened and looked downward. "I don't want to talk about that."

A trickle of relief washed through Clay. He wasn't ready to deal with that either. He was surprised by the guilt that followed that admission, though.

They walked in silence for a while before he decided to try again. "I've often wondered how your plans worked out."

"Not like they did in my dreams."

"No international travel? No feature on the network?"

"I did a lot of traveling. London, Nuremburg, Dubai…"

"Sounds exciting. And what about those political situations you wanted to cover?"

She glanced at him. "It was exciting, but I never rose above a glorified assistant. The work was much different than I'd envisioned. I could never find the groove, so to speak. I was homesick."

"For anyone in particular?"

"Mama Kay, Sandy." She met his gaze. "You. I didn't forget about you just because I left. Some things, some people, you never forget."

Clay's conscience nagged. He was being unfair. He knew more about her life than she realized. He should tell her the truth. She'd admitted she hadn't forgotten about him. Maybe he was still looking at their situation through his long-held resentment. He reached out and took her hand. "I haven't forgotten either."

As they walked along the riverbank, Clay continued to struggle with mixed emotions. Her explanation left out so much that he wanted to know. Why was she so thin and frail? What had put the sadness in her smile and taken the light of life from her golden-brown eyes?

Melody stopped and faced him. "Can I ask you a question?"

"I suppose it's your turn."

"Your wife… You must have fallen in love quickly after we broke up."

Clay's mind seized up. He was trapped. He struggled to find an answer that would sound reasonable. "I—um. It was a whirlwind thing."

"Like us?"

How was he supposed to answer that? If he said yes, she'd think he was a jerk who'd never really loved her, who'd fallen for the next woman to cross his path.

YOU pick your books –
WE pay for everything.
You get up to FOUR New Books ar
TWO Mystery Gifts...absolutely FR

Dear Reader,

I am writing to announce the launch of a huge **FREE BOO GIVEAWAY**... and to let you know that YOU are entitled t choose up to FOUR fantastic books that WE pay for.

Try **Love Inspired® Romance Larger-Print** books and fal in love with inspirational romances that take you on an uplifting journey of faith, forgiveness and hope.

Try **Love Inspired® Suspense Larger-Print** books where courage and optimism unite in stories of faith and love i the face of danger.

Or TRY BOTH!

In return, we ask just one favor: Would you please participate in our brief Reader Survey? We'd love to hea from you.

This FREE BOOKS GIVEAWAY means that we pay for *everything!* We'll even cover the shipping, and no purcha is necessary, now or later. So please return your survey today. You'll get **Two Free Books** and **Two Mystery Gifts** from each series to try, altogether worth over **$20!**

Sincerely

Pam Powers

Pam Powers
For Harlequin Reader Servi

Complete the survey below and return it today to receive up to 4 FREE BOOKS and FREE GIFTS guaranteed!

But if he said no, then the fake timeline he'd created would be shot.

"In a way."

"You must have loved her very much."

At least that was a question he could answer honestly. "I did. Very much."

"How did she die? Was she ill?"

Clay stopped walking. He had to end this. "I don't like to talk about it."

Melody touched his arm and gave it a sympathetic squeeze. "I'm sorry. I didn't mean to pry. It's just that Eli told me he's never seen a picture of his mom, and I wondered."

Clay stared at Melody. "He talked to you about his mother?"

"Yes. He said he wished he had a mom, and I told him about my mom dying when I was young. I thought maybe you could dig out a photo for him to look at."

"I don't have any. There aren't any."

Melody looked at him as if he'd lost his mind. Maybe he had. He'd been out of his mind when he'd concocted this situation, and now he was out of his mind trying to maintain it.

She studied him a moment longer, then smiled. "I need to get back to work. Thank you for the lunch. I'll talk to you later."

Before he could respond, she'd turned and hurried off down the walkway. She disappeared around the curve, leaving him too stunned to go after her.

Dragging his thumbnail across his eyebrow, he realized he'd have to clear up this mess soon before it exploded and everyone got hurt.

But he still had no idea how.

* * *

Melody arched her back, then stretched her arms over her head. She'd been poring over old newspapers for hours, caught up in the past, soaking in the imagery, immersing herself in the time period. She needed a break.

In the kitchen, she fixed a ham sandwich and added a few grapes and a cookie to her plate. Her thoughts whisked back to lunch with Clay a few days ago. Part of her had been glad to unburden her guilt and tell him about her life since they separated, though, of course, she'd touched on only a few things. He'd been searching for answers about the baby, but she couldn't deal with that. Not yet.

She had, however, enjoyed spending time with him. They'd talked and laughed, much like old times. She'd seen his easygoing side, even if it was still behind a shield of protection. His hesitation to discuss his wife puzzled her, though. She understood his reluctance, but there was something else there. Still, she'd found a new level of optimism after the encounter. Maybe, with time, they could at least become friends again. It was the most she could hope for.

Melody went back to work, lifting a large journal from one of Mrs. Temple's boxes. She took it and her glass of sweet tea into the living room. Barney jumped up on the sofa and nestled beside her as she opened the journal. *Walter Merritt*, the name of the newspaper editor, was clearly written on the inside. The first dozen pages were filled with notes about hiring employees, daily business notes and a few thoughts on how to improve circulation of the paper. Nothing of historical value that would benefit the book.

She turned the page and found a folded paper tucked into the seam. She pulled it out gingerly as the paper was yellow and brittle and the crease had small holes where it had already deteriorated. Carefully she spread open the page and scanned the text. It was the front page of the *Dispatch*, dated 1919. The lead article sent a chill through her veins. A photograph of the statue of Sergeant Linwood Croft was featured under a headline that declared "Local War Hero a Fraud."

Melody skimmed the few paragraphs, her heart stinging at the accusations laid forth. The implications were so far-reaching she had no idea what to do with them. Were the allegations true? If they were, then the town's beloved hero would be tarnished forever. But if they weren't true, why would someone print such a false report? What would they have to gain?

Mentally, she ran through her options and finally landed on the most logical course of action. Unfortunately, it was also the most uncomfortable. She needed to talk to Clay. Thankfully, he answered his phone.

"Are you busy?"

"Always. What's up?"

"I need some advice."

"Okay, shoot."

"No. I need you to come to the cottage." She ran a hand through her hair. "I've found something alarming. Something that could impact the whole town."

"Are you serious? What did you find? A terrorist cult or an underground sewing circle?"

"Clay, please. I need to see you. I don't know what to do." Her alarm must have finally registered because his tone shifted.

"Okay. I'll finish up and be there in half an hour."

Melody leaned back on the sofa and pulled Barney into her lap, her gaze zeroing in again on the old article on the coffee table. She hoped Clay would have a solution because no matter which way she looked at it, the outcome wasn't good.

When Clay finally knocked on the door, Melody had mentally tied herself into a dozen knots. She pulled open the door and glared. "What took you so long?"

Clay frowned. "I'm early. What's going on?"

She pointed to the paper on the coffee table. He reached to pick it up, but she stopped him. "It's too fragile to handle. Just read it and tell me what to do."

Clay eased onto the sofa and leaned over the document. Melody paced as he read, her nerves quivering.

"Well, what do you think?"

He held up his hand and kept reading. She wanted to scream.

When he finally leaned back, he looked as shell-shocked as she felt.

"What do I do?"

He shook his head. "Where did you find this?"

"In one of the journals Mrs. Temple gave me." She quickly explained about the boxes from the attic of the old home. "This article would have been printed when Walter Merritt was editor."

"Meaning?"

"I don't know. But it's a very disturbing accusation. What do I do about this? According to this article, Sergeant Linwood Croft wasn't the hero he was reported to be. He didn't take out a bunker of German soldiers—he wasn't even stationed in that area. How could this happen, and why hasn't it been revealed before?"

"No idea. I've lived here all my life and never heard

a word against our soldier. My grandpa or someone else in this town would have mentioned it if it were true."

"Our soldier?"

Clay grinned. "That's what everyone calls him. He's our hero. Our soldier." He leaned over the aged paper again. "It's obviously been printed in the local paper, so you'd assume it to be true, but…it would have to have come to light long before this."

Melody sat down in the armchair. "What do I do? Do I keep this secret, or do I put it in the book and destroy a local icon?"

Clay rubbed his chin. "I think the first thing we need to do is find out if it's true."

"Why wouldn't it be? It's been published. And it happened too long ago to find anyone who was alive who would remember. Is it some kind of conspiracy? Has the whole town turned a blind eye to this?"

Clay shook his head. "No. I can't see that happening. We need to find the entire edition that carried this article."

"Well, I haven't been through all the contents of the three boxes, but two of them are filled with old editions of the *Dispatch*. Maybe one of them is the right date."

"I'll check with my dad and see if he knows anything."

"Meanwhile, I'll talk to Deborah. As the librarian, she might have some information. And what about Jeffrey Hollis?"

Clay nodded. "He is our unofficial historian, though not all of his stories and information are reliable. He's a raconteur of sorts. He likes to tell tales that fit the occasion, if you know what I mean. Yeah, if there was anything to know, he'd be the one to ask." He stood up. "In the meantime, let's keep this under wraps. No one needs to know about this yet. It would just stir up trouble. It's probably nothing."

"Or something." Melody bit her lip. "Clay, this would shatter the town's very identity."

He squeezed her arm. "I know. We'll get to the bottom of it."

"Thanks. I was beside myself. I didn't know which way to turn."

"Glad I could help. I appreciate you coming to me first instead of—" He stopped.

"Of what?"

He shrugged. "You're a reporter at heart. You like to keep the public informed."

"Is that what you think of me? That I'd deliberately destroy Blessing's local hero for, for some kind of *notoriety*?" She crossed her arms and glared. "I've come to love this town and the people in it. I would never do something like that. You should know that by now."

Clay held her gaze. "I'm sorry. I shouldn't have said anything. I know you wouldn't stoop so low."

Her throat felt like she'd swallowed glass. "You'll never forgive me, will you?"

"What do you mean?"

"For leaving you and for giving—" She stopped, then started again. "For never getting in touch."

Clay broke eye contact. "That was a long time ago. I don't carry a grudge."

"Really? Feels like it to me."

He walked toward the door. "I'll see what I can find."

"Fine. So will I. I'll let you know if I learn anything."

"Same here."

Melody closed the door behind him, trying to ignore

the stinging in her chest. Clay would never trust her, never get over the way she'd treated him. She couldn't blame him, but she so wished they could clear the air and move forward.

Maybe it was time to talk about the baby. They'd danced around the topic. It hung in the air between them whenever they were together, yet neither one had the courage to address it. She was afraid that even if she told him the whole truth, he'd still resent her. She couldn't change the past. She could only pray that someday he'd forgive her, and she could forgive herself.

Melody studied Deborah's expression the next day as she sat in her office. She'd shared the old news article with the librarian in hopes she could shed some light on things. But Deborah was just as shocked as Clay had been.

"This is incredible. I've never heard any hint of this. No rumors about our soldier. I can't imagine an article like that being in the paper and not causing a riot."

"Are there any old newspapers stored here that we can sort through or someone who might know something from back then?"

"Jeffery Hollis might. He knows a lot of obscure tidbits about the town."

"Clay is checking with him, and I'm still going through the boxes Mrs. Temple gave me."

Deborah shook her head. "We've got to keep this to ourselves until we can uncover the truth. Something like this would tear Blessing apart."

"I agree. And I don't want to be the one to tell Blessing that their local hero is a fraud, that the man they've revered for over a hundred years wasn't a hero at all."

"It'd be like plunging a knife into the heart of this town. We don't have many famous people from here. North Mississippi has William Faulkner and Elvis Presley. We have our soldier and maybe that football star quarterback from a decade ago. The only other celebrity that hails from here is that writer fellow, Graham Napier."

"I see what you mean." Melody stood to leave. "Clay and I are still looking into this. We'll let you know if we learn anything."

Deborah removed her glasses and sighed. "I have a few resources I can check into, too. We need to get to the bottom of this."

Melody chewed her lip. "What if it's true and the soldier is a fraud?"

Deborah stood and squared her shoulders. "We'll cross that bridge when we come to it."

"Speaking of bridges…" Melody smiled. The librarian was a good woman to have on your side, but she knew someone even better. "I think that's where I'll go next. I need a visit to the bridge. I think the good Lord is the only one who can work this out."

Clay stood on the front porch, staring at the sun glinting on the pond. The day had started out so well. He'd fished in the pond before taking to the air and top cropping a longtime customer's fields with seeds. Then after lunch things had changed. Ben Clawson had called to tell him that he would no longer be using Dusty Birds's services. He was taking his business to Delta. No matter what Clay had offered it hadn't changed Ben's decision. He was regretful, and apologetic, but he had to do what was best for his farm.

Clay dragged a thumb across his eyebrow, then paced to the other end of the porch. He had no idea how he would give the news to his dad. Clawson was their largest and oldest customer. Dad and Ben had been friends for decades. Worse than that, losing the Clawson account put Dusty Birds in a precarious financial position.

"I thought I'd find you here."

Clay didn't look at his father as he came to his side. The only time Dad came looking for him was when he had something serious on his mind. "Just waiting on Eli to get home from school."

"Uh-huh. Sure. Well, then we have a few minutes to talk."

"What's on your mind, Dad?"

"I got a call from Ben Clawson earlier today. He wanted to make sure I understood why he was taking his business elsewhere."

Clay set his jaw. He'd specifically asked Ben to keep this to himself until he could tell his dad. He should have gone to his dad as soon as they'd finished talking, but he'd needed time to find the right words. He glanced at his parent. "Yeah, I was going to tell you."

"When you found a way to spin it so it didn't sound so bad?"

Clay leaned against the porch post. He never could fool his dad. He always saw through any falsehood he attempted. "I didn't want you to be upset."

"Son, I'm not going to have a stroke every time I hear bad news. That being said, I am concerned about what losing the Clawson account will do to our company." He paused, then looked directly at Clay. "I looked at the books. I know how serious things are."

Clay's heart sank. He'd tried so hard to keep the

news from his dad. It was all out in the open now. "I'm working on a solution, Dad. If the weather holds and we can meet all our contracts, we'll make it through this season."

Dad nodded. "True, but there's more rain in the forecast. What then?"

"I thought we could sell the Air Tractor. There's a market for that plane. It should sell quickly."

"No." Dave clamped his hands around the railing with a loud slap. "That plane is our workhorse. I'd sooner sell the other two. What about letting Jared go?"

Clay shook his head. "He's already agreed to a reduction in pay, but he's got a baby on the way."

He looked up at the squeak of air brakes. The school bus had pulled up at the end of the drive. Eli hopped down the steps and jogged toward the house.

Dad patted his shoulder. "We'll work it out, son. Don't worry."

Clay set his concerns aside as Eli hurried up the porch steps, a big smile on his face.

"Hey, Dad."

Clay ruffled his son's hair, the same shade as Melody's. "Hey to you. How was school?"

Eli shrugged. "Good. Oh, look, Miss Melody is leaving. I wanted to help her this afternoon. I don't have homework. I could take lots of pictures."

"She probably won't be gone long."

"Dad, I want to get Miss Melody a rocking chair."

"What? Why?"

"She likes to sit on the porch, but she doesn't have a chair."

"Oh." He thought about the times he'd gone to the cottage and found her sitting on the steps. It worked on a nice day but not when it was raining. "I think that rocker Grandma liked so much is in the shed behind the cottage. We'll get it out and she can use that."

Eli smiled. "Cool. She'll be really happy."

Clay was torn between pride for his son's thoughtfulness and concern that Eli was growing fond of Melody. Secretly he hoped Eli would forget about the idea, but that notion was dashed quickly.

"Can we get it now since she's not home? We can surprise her when she gets back."

Together they trudged down to the shed. The rocker was stored right inside the door along with a few other pieces of outdoor furniture and a small grill. He'd let Melody know they were there. She might like to use them.

The rocker was heavier than Clay remembered, but with Eli's help they wrangled it up onto the cottage porch. They added a small table beside it.

Eli smiled with delight. "She'll be really happy."

Clay gave his son a quick hug. "She'll be very thankful for your thoughtfulness. I'm proud of you, son."

Eli was silent a long moment. "Can I ask you something, Dad?"

"Of course."

"What did my mom look like? Was she pretty? Did she have brown hair or blond?"

The pounding in Clay's heart surged to his ears. The moment he'd dreaded had finally arrived. He wasn't prepared to answer his questions. Ever.

"What brought this on?"

Eli shrugged. "You never talk about her, and I want to know. How did she die? Was she sick or was it an accident?"

"Has something happened to bring this all up?"

"Not really. Toby Unger's mom died from cancer. I wanted to know how mine died."

"I see."

Eli leaned on the porch rail, staring at the cottage. "Was she as nice as Miss Melody? I think she'd be a great mom, don't you?"

Clay's throat was so constricted he could only nod. He was living a nightmare.

"Dad. Do you have a picture of my mom?"

"No, Eli. I'm sorry. I don't have any pictures."

His shoulders sagged in disappointment. "Oh. Miss Melody doesn't have any of her mom either."

"You talked about your mom with Miss Melody?"

Eli nodded. "She understands not having a mom. Did you know she had a bunch of foster families? They weren't very nice to her."

He had to end this conversation. "If you don't have any homework, then how about a flying lesson?"

"Really? All right!" Eli's eyes lit up and he darted off toward the house.

Clay let out a deep breath. At least for the next hour, he wouldn't have to think about his secrets.

Chapter Eight

Melody knew something was different as soon as she pulled up at the cottage, but it took a moment to see the new addition to her porch. A lovely old rocker had been placed there with a small table beside. She touched it, impressed at the smooth wood. She lowered herself into the chair and reveled at how it fit her body perfectly—as if it had been made for her. The rocking motion was smooth and soothing, and she closed her eyes enjoying the movement.

Who had put it here? Dave? Clay? Doubtful. The old Clay would have done something this thoughtful, but the man she'd known here in Blessing probably wouldn't have done this.

"Hey, Miss Melody."

She opened her eyes to see Eli racing toward her on his bike.

"Do you like your rocking chair? It was in the shed and me and Dad got it out for you."

Her heart swelled. *Of course.* "Oh, Eli. I love it so much. I'll be out here all the time now. I might not get any work done." He giggled and hopped off his bike.

She stood and went to him, giving him a big hug. "You are such a nice young man. Thank you for thinking about me."

He blushed and smiled. "You're welcome."

Eli's thoughtfulness buoyed her through the next day and gave her a welcome respite from the tedious research about Sergeant Croft. Clay had called a short while ago and told her he was coming over. Hopefully, he had good news.

Melody answered the door before Clay stopped knocking. "Hi. How did it go today?"

Clay shook his head. "Not much to report. I spoke with Jeffrey. He remembers hearing a story his grandma told about a mysterious article that was supposed to have been printed but never was."

"About the soldier?"

"He wasn't sure. He's going to do some digging and get back to me. How about you?"

"I met with Deborah, but she'd never heard anything about a claim that the soldier wasn't really a hero. We've agreed to keep this to ourselves for now. I need to go through the rest of the items in that box. There might an answer there."

"I'm free this evening. It'll go faster with the two of us."

"Good idea. Oh, and thank you for the rocker. I've enjoyed it very much."

Clay smiled. "I'm glad, but it was all Eli's idea. I just helped him drag it out of the shed."

"It's the most comfortable rocker I've ever used."

"It was made by a local man. Rockers are his specialty. He made one for the governor last year."

Melody brought one of the boxes from her office and

placed it on the coffee table. "Have you eaten? I was going to put a pizza in the oven."

"Mmm, that sounds good. We can eat and research at the same time."

She wagged a finger at him. "As long as you don't get any cheese on the papers."

The boxes proved to be a treasure trove of information perfect for the book, but nothing turned up to explain the news article. "There are still some papers at the bottom of the second box. Maybe they'll turn up something."

Clay stood and picked up his empty glass. "Divide them in half and we'll tackle that next."

A tattered envelope lay on top inside the box. Melody lifted it out, and her heart started racing as she saw what was underneath. "Clay, there are more old newspapers in here!"

Clay retuned and sat down. "How old?"

She grinned. "1914 to 1920. The answer might be right here." He smiled back at her. It felt good to have a common goal, a shared experience. It was much nicer than the animosity that had hovered over them since she'd come to Blessing.

Clay spread his stack on the breakfast table, while Melody used the large coffee table. They worked silently as they carefully read through the old papers.

Suddenly Clay shouted, "Melody! I've got it."

She jumped up and hurried to the kitchen, her heart filled with expectation. Clay smiled over his shoulder. "June 10, 1919. Right?"

"Yes." She stood close, and they peered down at the paper. Their joy quickly faded, however, as they scanned the front page. The lead story was about a downtown fire that had destroyed a retail store.

"I don't understand," Melody said. "This is the right date. Where's the article about our soldier?"

Clay grinned, a twinkle in his eyes. "You're calling him your soldier now, too?"

Her cheeks warmed. "I'm a resident of Blessing. I'm allowed."

"Yes, you are." Clay carefully turned the rest of the pages of the edition but found nothing about Sergeant Croft.

Melody sank into a chair. "I don't understand. If you had this kind of knowledge and printed up the article, why not publish it?"

"I don't know." Clay closed the paper, folded it carefully and placed it back on the stack. "But…we have a copy that was printed. This doesn't make sense. Maybe we should check the rest of the papers. The date could have been wrong."

"I don't think so." Melody rubbed her lip. "Something else is going on here."

"Like what? What reason could anyone have for printing up an article like this, only to leave it out of the paper?"

"Maybe it wasn't true," Melody suggested.

"Then we need to find out."

"I will. Until I do, we still need to keep this quiet. I don't want to upset the town."

Clay touched her left arm and gently squeezed it. She managed to mask the sting it caused.

"Neither do I. We'll find the answer. It just might take a while."

She nodded. "Online records for the military are

available," she mused. "And if that doesn't work, I know a few people I can call on for a favor."

Clay grinned. "Ah. Some of your international connections, no doubt?"

She looked away, crossing her arms over her chest. "In a way." What would he say if she told him her contact was the only other survivor of the Shanghai bombing?

"Sorry. I shouldn't tease you. I'd better go."

He walked to the door and she followed, a sense of loss settling over her shoulders. She liked having him in her cozy cottage. She liked having him close. Foolish, but there it was. Her heart still held a deep affection for him. They'd shared too much. The bond was too strong.

"Will you ask Eli to come over tomorrow? He can start photographing these papers. I'd like a record of everything before I donate them."

"Sure. He likes working with you. He's even asked for a camera for his birthday."

"I like working with him, too. He's a very sweet young man. I'm still in awe of his thoughtfulness in finding me the rocker."

The smile on Clay's face faded and a muscle in his jaw twitched. Was he jealous of his son's time with her? She could understand that. If Eli were her son, she'd be jealous of any time he spent with someone else.

Melody watched Clay walk across the lawn and into the house before she closed the door. He was such an elegant man. She never grew tired of watching him. His masculine stride, the roll of his shoulders as he moved, never failed to bring a warmth to her heart.

No time for that now. She had serious research to conduct. She had to uncover the truth about that article, and she prayed it wouldn't be true. The last thing she wanted in this world was to shatter Blessing's pride in its hero.

Clay stopped in the doorway of Melody's office a few days later, taking a moment to watch her at work. Her gaze was focused on the computer screen, a small frown furrowed her brow and her lips were pressed into a tight line. He smiled. Even deep in concentration she was lovely to look at. She was the most fascinating woman he'd ever met, and no matter what he told himself, she still held a special place in his heart.

He hated to interrupt her, but they had agreed to meet with Deborah at the library this morning. He knocked on the door frame. She glanced up, her golden-brown eyes focused, then warmed with a smile.

"Good morning. I'm almost ready."

"Discover anything useful?"

"Not yet. Nothing much online except for Croft's birth certificate and his enlistment card. I found the information about his heroics and it confirms what we've always believed. I called my friend in Washington. He said he'll dig into it and get back to me. How about you?"

"Nope. Nothing important." He took a seat in the chair opposite her desk and stretched out his legs. "I did find out that our soldier was part of a love triangle."

Melody's eyes lit up. "Who with? Did you get a name?"

Clay frowned. "No. Why would I? It's just an old rumor."

Melody stood and picked up her purse. "Maybe, maybe not. Love has been the source of all kinds of

strange behaviors. Let's go see what our friendly neigh-
borhood librarian might have learned."

Clay opened the annex door for her, and they started
down the block toward the library. As they neared the
hardware store, a man stepped out and blocked their
way. Clay instinctively placed himself in front of Melody. He recognized the man as Fred Odell, a local car-
penter known for his short temper.

"Good day, Fred. Something on your mind?"

The man pointed his finger at Melody. "She is. How
dare you make up lies about our soldier." He gestured
toward the statue across the street in the park, then
glared at Melody. "He was a war hero. He saved dozens
of lives. He should be honored, not have his reputation
dragged through the mud by someone who isn't even
from here. You're an outsider. You have no right." He
took a step toward her, and Clay placed a hand on his
chest to hold him back.

"What are you talking about?"

"Her dirty claims that Sergeant Croft is a fraud. It's
all in the paper."

Clay glanced at Melody. She looked as puzzled as
he was. "The paper?"

"Come on, Reynolds. Don't you read the newspaper?"

Fred had exhausted much of his anger. He huffed out
a breath but had one final shot before he turned to go.
"You should go back where you came from, lady. We
don't need you here."

Clay sensed Melody shaking beside him and slipped
his arm around her shoulders. "I'm sorry about that."

"What was he talking about? I haven't told anyone
about that article. Except Deborah. Did you?"

"Only my dad and Jeffery. Neither of them would talk."

Melody started forward. "We need to look at the paper."

Clay pulled a few coins from his pocket, inserted them into the dispenser at the end of the block and pulled out the latest issue of the *Banner*. The photo on the front page was of the old article Melody had discovered. The headline read "Local Hero a Liar."

Melody covered her mouth. "Oh, Clay. This is awful. How could this have happened?"

"I don't know. Let's get to the library. Maybe Deborah knows something." Clay held Melody's elbow as they hurried across the street and up the steps to the library. A middle-aged woman confronted them the moment they stepped inside the old building. Her scowl was directed at Melody.

"You're supposed to be writing a history of Blessing to make us proud, Miss Williams. Not using your research to demean our cherished citizens." She marched off before either of them could respond.

Clay took Melody's hand. "Don't worry. We'll fix this."

"I don't see how now. I've ruined everything. I should have left that article in the journal and ignored it."

"No. You're not cut out that way."

"Thank you. I appreciate your confidence in me."

The meeting with the librarian provided no new information. Deborah had been in meetings and had just learned of the article being leaked.

Their next stop was the newspaper office. Clay's anger was building, and he hoped Aaron McCoy, the current editor of the *Banner*, had a good explanation.

He marched into the office not waiting for an invitation. "I want to know where you got that article about our soldier."

Aaron glanced up, unfazed by Clay's challenge. "A source."

"What source? Who gave it to you?"

"Can't tell you. You know that."

"Aaron, there's no proof that article is even true. It's over a hundred years old. Why would you print something so explosive?"

"It sells papers."

Clay huffed out a frustrated breath and set his hands on his hips. "So you don't care if the information is true or not?"

Aaron stood and straightened his tie, a smug look on his round face. "Not really."

Clay took a step closer to the man, towering over his smaller stature. "I thought you loved this town."

"I do." He sighed and sat down. "Maybe you should have had a talk with your son before you let him spill the beans."

"What are you talking about?"

"Your Eli told my Parker about this old article saying the soldier wasn't really a hero. Parker didn't believe him, so he gave him a copy of the photo. I saw it. I printed it."

"What happened to verifying before you publish?"

Aaron shrugged. "It's business. Not personal."

Clay took Melody's arm and steered her from the building. "I can't believe Eli would do this. Did you tell him to keep the article a secret?"

Melody touched her forehead. "I don't think so. It

never occurred to me he'd tell anyone. Why would he care? He's ten."

"How did he get a copy of the—oh." Clay dragged his thumbnail across his brow. "He's taking pictures of all the articles."

Melody lowered her head. "Oh, Clay. I never thought of that. I'm so sorry."

He shook his head. "It's no one's fault. But we'll have to work overtime now to get to the bottom of this."

Melody's eyes grew moist. "First, the town hates me and now I've gotten Eli in trouble. I never meant for this to happen. I'm so sorry. I love this town and I love Eli."

She looked so vulnerable and sweet. He pulled her into his arms. "It's not your fault. You did everything right."

She pulled away. "You must hate me. I've placed Eli in a horrible position. He's going to feel awful about this. Please don't punish him."

"Of course not. But we will have a long father-and-son talk. I think he probably got caught up in the situation and didn't realize the consequences. He's just a boy."

He dropped his gaze to their clasped hands. A tingle ran up his spine. He remembered another time when they'd stood this way, under a shady tree with low branches that provided a shield from onlookers and a private place to steal a kiss.

Was she remembering, too? Did he want her to? He did. The realization rattled his peace of mind.

His mouth suddenly went dry. He released her hands and stepped back. "I need to go. I have a job this morning."

She gave him a small, understanding smile. "And I

have a meeting with another longtime resident. If she still wants to talk to me. I'm sure everyone in town has seen that article."

Clay pointed a finger at her and smiled. "You stay strong. Don't let anyone bully you. This is all speculation."

"I will. I can be tough when I need to be. I can take care of myself."

"I know. You're very good at it."

Clay walked to his car and slid behind the wheel. This morning hadn't turned out the way he'd hoped. He'd looked forward to spending time with Melody at the library. He liked having a project together. There was the book, of course, but she'd mainly handled that on her own, calling on him only when she needed an introduction to someone. But digging into the truth about Sergeant Croft, investigating the mystery, comparing notes and sharing new information had brought them closer. He'd worried about Eli missing her when she left, but now he began to worry that he might, too. He couldn't afford those feelings.

Melody's heart was breaking. Clay had brought Eli over to the cottage to discuss the news article. He looked so small sitting at the table that she just wanted to hug him. But this was Clay's area, not hers. She couldn't help wondering what it would be like to be a parent, to love your child more than anything and yet have to discipline them for their own good.

Eli glanced from her to his dad, sensing the serious mood. "Am I in trouble?"

Clay shook his head. "No. We do need to talk to you about something you did, though."

"I did my chores, honest. And I fed Lady."

"It's not that. It's about the photo you gave Parker. The one of the article about our soldier."

Eli swallowed and glanced between them. "I made another copy for Miss Melody to keep."

"Can you tell me how you and Parker started talking about it?"

Eli shrugged. "I was telling him about the cool camera I got to use and how I sort the photos for Miss Melody so she can find them when she puts the book together."

"Go on."

"He said he didn't believe me. I told him about the old articles and how yellow and flaky they are and how the special setting I use on the camera makes them better."

Melody met Clay's gaze. The situation was becoming clear. Clay rested his forearms on the table and leaned toward his son.

"So you wanted to prove to him that what you were saying was true. Why did you show him that article and not the other photos?"

Eli squirmed in his chair. "I just took it that morning. I showed him after school. He liked that it was about our soldier. We all know about him."

Melody sensed it was time to leave the two alone. "I need to take Barney for a walk. I'll be back shortly." Clay gave her a grateful nod.

She stayed close to the cottage, keeping an eye on the door and praying Clay wouldn't be too hard on the boy. He'd had no idea that sharing that photo would cause trouble. She knew he must feel awful about what he'd done. Her heart ached for him.

When her door finally opened, Eli emerged first, hands in pockets, head bowed. He trudged across the lawn toward home. Melody searched Clay's face for a clue to the outcome of his father-son talk.

"How is he?"

"Upset. He feels really bad. And angry at Parker."

"Did you punish him?"

"No. But I did stress how important it is for an employee to guard the information of his employer."

She smiled at the twinkle in Clay's eyes. "So he can still help me? I really like having him around." Clay's eyes clouded.

"I guess. He seems to enjoy it."

"Would you object to me paying him a small amount each week? Whatever you think appropriate." He took a long time answering but finally nodded.

"I'll think about it and let you know."

"Good. In the meantime I need to get back to work and see what else I can find out about our soldier."

"Right. We still have a powder keg to defuse. Only finding the truth will stop it."

Melody saw Eli trudging toward the cottage from across the drive the next afternoon. His shoulders were slumped and his hands were in his pockets. His dejected body language touched her heart. Poor boy. Apparently, he was still burdened with remorse for sharing the news article. She was determined to make his first day back with her as pleasant as possible. The thought of him feeling responsible bothered her deeply.

She raised her hand and waved when he looked at her. His half-hearted response made her sad. She smiled as he tromped up onto the porch. "I was hoping you'd come today. I have a lot of pictures for you to take."

"You still want me to do that after—"

"Of course. That wasn't your fault. I should have explained the situation to you."

"You're not mad at me?"

"No. But I think it best if we keep our work here to ourselves. At least until this thing with the article is cleared up."

Eli nodded. "Okay."

They went inside and Eli started toward the spare room, where he did most of his work. "Miss Melody, I'm really sorry. I didn't mean to get you into trouble. I would never do that."

Melody saw the glint in his blue eyes and her heart melted. "Oh, Eli. I understand." She pulled him into a hug. "It was an innocent mistake. We've all made them. We learn from them and do better the next time."

Eli's shoulders sagged. "I'll bet you never did anything this dumb. You're smart and you've been all over the world."

She laughed ruefully. "I've made so many mistakes it would take the rest of my life to list them all."

He smiled up at her. "I'm glad you're not mad. I like being here and taking the pictures for you. I like you."

"I like you, too, Eli. If I had a son, I'd want him to be just like you."

"I wish you were my mom."

Melody's breath caught in her throat. It took her a second to find her voice. "Oh, Eli. That's the nicest compliment I've ever received. Thank you. I would be honored to be your mother." She gave him a hug relishing the moment.

She would never have this feeling again.

Chapter Nine

Clay glanced over at Melody, who was leaning close to the window of his Cessna and taking pictures of Blessing below. She'd been so excited about flying over his hometown and taking photographs. She claimed her plans for including the aerial shots in the Blessing history book would give the locals a whole new perspective of their lovely town.

With each pass over Blessing, she had spotted another landmark, and her joy had brought a happy giggle as she snapped a barrage of pictures. He had to admit he was enjoying being her pilot guide. He'd been reluctant at first, but now he was glad he'd agreed. It was like the adventures they used to have when they were together.

He found himself wishing he could keep on flying, enjoying her laughter and the closeness. But he had obligations.

He taxied and stopped the plane in its usual spot, then shut down the engine. He smiled over at Melody. She was so close he could see her pulse beating in her neck. He cleared his throat. "Did you get everything you need for the book?"

She smiled broadly, her eyes sparkling. "Oh, yes. More than I expected. Thank you for taking me up."

"You're welcome." He swallowed around the tightness in his throat. "If you need to go up again, just let me know."

"Thanks, but I doubt I'll need to. My biggest problem now will be which photos to use."

"How's the book coming?" He didn't really care, but he wasn't ready to end their time together. His feelings for Melody were growing despite his attempts to halt them. When it came to her, he was weak. His heart took over every time.

"Wonderfully. I have the first draft of the text all worked out. Of course, I need to edit it a few more times. I keep finding new tidbits I want to include, but I can't use all the research I've collected. The book would be two thousand pages long."

He smiled and watched as her excitement illuminated her being.

She brushed her hair from her cheek. "I wish I could put all the family histories and all the anecdotes and cherished memories into the book. The residents are so proud of their heritage and their contributions to the town. It would be nice for them to be able to share their stories with everyone."

She stopped and stared at him, her eyes wide. "Oh! I just had an idea. What if someone started a blog about Blessing? It could be a place where people could go online and read each other's histories and share their own."

"We have a website for the city."

She nodded. "I know, but this would be different, interactive so people could add to it." She reached over and laid her hand on his arm. "Clay, there are so many sweet and inspiring stories that need to be shared. It needs to be special."

Her enthusiasm had her vibrating with life and energy. More than he'd seen since she'd arrived in town.

"Sounds like a big job. And many of our residents are older and don't use the internet."

"I know, but I could work around that."

"You could?"

She blushed and lowered her gaze. "I'm sorry. I know I get carried away. I like the idea but someone else will have to do it. I'll be gone in a few weeks." She reached for the door handle. "Thanks again, Clay. I really enjoyed flying with you."

The realization that Melody would be leaving soon lodged like a stone in his chest. Instead of being relieved that her stay was ending, he found himself wishing there was more time. He wanted to straighten things out between them. He wanted, no, he *needed* to tell her the truth about Eli. The secret was gnawing at him more every day. His father was right. He couldn't keep this up. It would destroy him.

Clay climbed out of the cockpit, relieved to have some distance between him and Melody. Being in the air, in the cramped space of his aircraft, he had been too close to her for comfort. As much as he wanted to deny it, being near her dredged up all his old feelings. Feelings he'd ignored for a long time. He walked around to the other side of the plane to help Melody out, but she was already standing on the wing. As she made the small jump onto the ground, the sleeve of her blouse caught on something and ripped open. She gasped and grabbed her left arm, trying to pull the fabric back into place. Emotion filled her eyes and she turned away, but not before he saw her bare arm covered in horrific scars.

His throat seized up. What had happened to her? "Melody?"

She kept her back to him, retrieving her camera and small backpack while still trying to cover her arm. He took her right hand and gently turned her toward him. "What happened?"

She pulled away, her eyes lowered, but he could see her lip quivering. His heart filled with an icy chill. The thought of her being seriously injured was intolerable. He may have issues with her behavior, but he never wanted her to suffer. The scars told a story of great pain and he had to know what had caused it.

"It's nothing. It's old news."

He couldn't take his eyes from the horror of her scars. All he wanted to do was hold her close and protect her from harm. "Melody. Please. I need to know."

The pain in her eyes turned to determination. "Life."

"What does that mean?" She stood quiet and rigid for a long while. He wondered if she would tell him or not. Finally, she spoke, her voice so soft he had to lean closer to hear her.

"My last assignment was in Shanghai with a world news agency."

"Your big dream."

She shook her head, looking at her hands. "I was an assistant news editor, hardly the star. There was a lot of unrest over human rights issues and a certain faction was against us being there. They…they set off a bomb in our hotel offices."

Clay exhaled a groan. "Melody."

"I don't remember much before waking up in the

hospital. My arm and shoulder had third-degree burns. I had a severe concussion and several other injuries. I didn't get to go home for several months."

Clay's mind did a quick inventory of past events. Something about her story rang a bell. "How long ago was this?"

"Two years."

His heart skipped a beat. "The International Shanghai Hotel? I remember reading about it. That was a terrible tragedy."

"We lost so many. Only two of us survived." She swiped at her tears. "My best friend didn't make it."

Clay attempted to draw her into his arms, but she resisted. She was still attempting to cover her scars. He took her hand instead.

She shook her head. "Don't look. I'm so ugly."

"No. You could never be ugly." He tugged her close, wrapping his arms around her, careful not to brush against her scars for fear of causing pain. When she relaxed against him, he kissed the top of her head, then rested his cheek on her silky hair. The gesture unleashed a torrent of tears that quickly became sobs. He held her, praying for some way to comfort her, asking the Lord to heal her pain.

Slowly her crying eased, but he kept her close, her head resting against his chest and over his heart. His mind told him it was where she belonged. Always.

If only…

Melody lifted her head, her brown eyes glistening with remnants of her tears. Their eyes locked, and for a brief moment they were back in time. They were in love and happy. He remembered her kisses. Her lips parted and he lowered his head.

What would it hurt? One small kiss. Not of passion but of comfort.

"Clay."

She breathed his name and reality crashed in around him. He touched her chin with his fingertips, then kissed her cheek. He couldn't claim her kiss yet. Not until he told her the truth.

The warmth in Melody's eyes faded and she stepped away.

Clay secured the plane, then helped her to his car. "Would you like to go somewhere and get a bite to eat?"

"No. I want to go home."

Her tone held a harshness he'd never heard before. She huddled near the door, staring out the window as he drove to the cottage. He walked her to the door. She grasped the knob, then paused, looking over her shoulder. "Could you stay for a while? I don't want to be alone."

"Of course." Her request surprised him. He'd expected her to hurry inside. He wasn't sure what to do or how to help her. Did she want to talk or did she simply need a quiet companion for a while? He stood inside the door as she placed her backpack and camera on the chair.

"I'll be right back, I want to…" She tugged on her sleeve.

When she returned a few minutes later, she was wearing a fresh shirt with long sleeves. She curled up on the sofa. He took a seat at the other end. "Can I get you something to drink?"

She shook her head. "I'm fine."

Clay studied her eyes, now filled with regret. "Why didn't you tell me?"

She tucked her hair behind her ear. "No one wants to see my scars. I don't even like to look at them."

"It wouldn't have mattered to me."

"Maybe not, but you would have asked questions, wanted an explanation. It's easier to keep myself covered. It spares everyone embarrassment."

"Is this the life event you've referred to? The one that changed you?"

She nodded, staring at her hands a long while before continuing. "I was so confident that I could direct my life. That I was in control. Only nothing went the way I'd planned. The opportunities never came. The positions I applied for never opened up. The Shanghai job was my last hope."

"I don't remember you being low on hope. You always saw the bright side of things."

She gave him a small smile. "I find my hope elsewhere now, thanks to Mama Kay. She led me to faith. But you're right. The bombing changed everything. My best friend, Rachel, had just turned up the volume on her phone because her favorite song was playing. It had become an office joke. Most of us hated the song, so she did it just to tease us. She glanced over her shoulder at me and then—"

Melody shifted and rested one hand at her throat. "I heard that song the day of the porch crawl when I was waiting for you, and—"

"It triggered a flashback."

"How did you know?"

"My uncle Paul suffers from PTSD. He has moments like that occasionally. I'm sorry you had to go through that. I wish I could help somehow." He hated feeling useless.

She shrugged. "This is just something I have to do myself."

"I get that. But you can still go after your dream, you know."

"No." She picked up a pillow and clutched it to her chest. "I was failing at that job. I wasn't cut out for the international news corps. I ended up here because it's taken me two years to get back to a relatively normal life, mentally and physically. I needed a job I was reasonably sure I could complete successfully. The Blessing history book was the perfect solution and Blessing the perfect place since Sandy was here for moral support." She met his gaze. "I'm still learning about the new me. The one who looks at life differently, more compassionately. The way you always did."

Clay looked away. He'd been lacking in that area toward Melody. He rubbed his hands together. "Melody, there's something I need to tell you."

Her eyes grew wide and she pushed up from the sofa. "Not right now, Clay. Please. I'm tired. I want to lie down. It's been a…busy morning. Can it wait?"

Clay stood. "Sure. I need to get to work." He started toward the door, then took one last glance at her. She'd wrapped her arms protectively around her waist. Her eyes were moist in her pale face. He wanted to go to her again and hold her close, but he knew this wasn't the time.

He turned and left the cottage. He had a lot to think about. Melody truly had changed, and he needed to reassess his assumptions about her.

Melody took her coffee onto the front porch the next morning and sat in the wooden rocker. Sandy smiled patiently from the wicker chair Melody had added. She'd called her sister first thing and asked her to come over for a heart-to-heart.

"What's going on that you need to talk so early in the morning?"

Melody held her cup between her palms, allowing the gentle sway of the rocker and warmth of the caffeine to calm her anxiety. "Clay saw my scars yesterday."

Sandy's lips formed a silent *oh*. "I see. And what did he say?"

"He hugged me."

"I guess that means he didn't run away screaming in horror."

Melody had to smile at that. Sandy knew it was her greatest fear that people would see her damaged arm and turn away in disgust. "No. He was upset that I'd been hurt. He was sweet and compassionate."

"Did you tell him the whole story?"

She nodded. "He was shocked and concerned. We, uh, almost kissed."

Sandy leaned forward. "Really? Maybe I wasn't so wrong after all."

"What are you talking about? Wrong about what?"

"I've noticed a change in your attitude the last few weeks, and a softer tone in your voice when you talk about Clay. I think you're falling in love with him again." She shrugged. "And it sounds like the feeling might be mutual."

Melody waved off the observation. "No. That's not happening."

"Why not? You said it was love at first sight. Maybe that kind of love doesn't die over time."

"It did for Clay. We've developed a working relationship but that's all. Besides, now that he knows, he'll only feel pity for me."

Sandy rolled her eyes. "You don't know that. I don't know Clay well, but I know he's a man with a kind heart. He wouldn't pity you. He'd more likely admire your strength."

She had a point. Clay would never feel sorry for her. Melody had sensed his concern and his sadness over her ordeal, but she hadn't sensed pity. Of course, he hadn't followed through on that kiss. She'd wanted him to, desperately, but at the last minute he'd kissed her cheek instead. What did it mean?

On the ride back to her cottage, she'd been anxious to be alone, yet when they'd arrived, she couldn't face the emptiness of her home and asked him to stay. His presence gave her comfort, and she'd confessed more to him than she'd intended.

Melody pressed her lips together. "He said he had something to tell me."

"What?"

"I don't know. I got scared and told him I was tired. I was afraid he was going to ask me to leave or stop work on the book or not to see Eli anymore."

"That's silly. None of that makes any sense."

"I know but I got this sick feeling in the pit of my stomach and I panicked." She rubbed the side of her cup with her thumb. "I'm afraid he's going to ask me about the baby, and I don't think I can ever explain my decision to him. He's a family man. A great father. He wouldn't understand."

"Sweetie, you need to talk to him about that." Sandy squeezed her hand. "You need to tell him everything for both your sakes. Then, whatever the outcome, you can move on. I know you feel guilty, but you have to deal with this. And the sooner the better."

Melody mulled over Sandy's advice later that afternoon. She knew her sister was right but the thought of confessing to Clay was terrifying. Thankfully, she had her work on the book. It gave her an escape from her thoughts, and researching Sergeant Croft's military history was keeping her glued to the internet.

"Knock. Knock. Can I interrupt?"

Melody smiled as Dave strolled into her office. "Please. I can use a break."

Dave took a seat. "How's your probing into our soldier coming along?"

It was the one topic she wished he hadn't brought up. She smiled before biting her lip. "I heard from my friend in DC, and he confirms that Sergeant Croft was definitely where he was reported to be and he did, in fact, take out that machine-gun bunker." She hesitated.

Dave raised his brows. "But? Is there something wrong?"

"There are a few small discrepancies with the dates on his commendation. One source says it was awarded July 17. Another lists the date as July 27."

"What does that mean?"

"I'm not sure yet. Probably just a clerical error."

"What about that article? Any progress on why it was published and what it might mean?"

She shook her head. "Not yet, but I'm still digging through the old papers and files."

Dave rubbed his chin. "I'm sorry to hear that. It makes what I'm about to tell you more difficult."

Melody held her breath. Dave never had bad news. He was always upbeat and positive.

"The city council is concerned about the article and how it will impact the community, especially with the bicentennial on the horizon. We're trying to present a positive image of Blessing. Having our soldier's honor in doubt could be problematic."

Melody tried to put all the reassurance in her voice as possible. "I'm doing all I can. I *will* get to the bottom of this."

Dave smiled. "I know you will. However, the council would like to meet with you. They have questions about this whole thing."

"I don't understand. Do they think I'm lying? That I want to destroy Croft's reputation?"

"No, but I think they would like some reassurance that you are trying to solve the issue and not use it to your advantage somehow."

"That's ridiculous. How would smearing Croft's image help me?"

Dave leaned forward. "Melody, I have no doubts about your intentions or your findings, and I know you're working hard to get answers. But the council only sees that a stranger came to Blessing and found some dirt on our hero. They're upset and angry."

Melody crossed her arms. "Don't I know it. I can hardly go anywhere lately without someone giving me a dirty look or telling me to go home."

"I'm sorry. That's not the tone we want to present to visitors, especially those who have come to help us."

"What does the council want me to do?"

"They want you to attend the meeting this week and bring them up to speed. They'll probably ask how you found the article, how it got into our local paper and what you're doing to solve the problem."

"Okay. I can do that. I have all the information and documentation on what I've been doing. I'm sure I can reassure them."

Dave straightened. "I hope so. Because there are a few members who have suggested that your contract for the book should be voided."

She couldn't believe what she'd heard. "They want me fired? But the book is almost done. It's supposed to go to the printer in a week. All I have to do is run through it once more and adjust a few pictures." She sighed. "And, of course, explain about our soldier. I would like that cleared before I finish."

Dave smiled. "Don't worry. I'll do everything in my power to prevent you losing your job. I have some clout in this town. Just make sure you have everything at your fingertips for the meeting."

"I will."

Melody cradled her head in her hands after Dave left. Maybe coming to Blessing hadn't been such a good idea after all. Seeing Clay again, meeting Eli and now the mess with the soldier—it was all taking a toll on her sanity. *Lord, give me strength.*

Straightening her back, she looked at her computer screen. She'd search again. One thing she'd learned through all her trials was that the only way to deal with adversity was to go through it. There was no going around.

Pulling up her files on Sergeant Croft, she started from the beginning. There had to be an explanation somewhere. She wasn't going to stop until she found it. She refused to let the people of Blessing down.

Chapter Ten

Clay stretched his legs in front of him, his gaze following the ripples on the pond in front of his home. Mentally he told himself he was fishing, but his pole lay beside him in the grass. Learning of Melody's ordeal and seeing those horrible scars on her arm had made him sick to his stomach. Since then, he'd gone through a full range of emotions from anger at the terrorist who thought bombing a news office would solve anything to aching with sadness for Melody for having to endure so much.

He'd had to take a step back and reassess his ideas about Melody. For years, he'd clung to the notion that she was selfish and that she was indestructible. But she wasn't. His dad was right. She was broken and vulnerable, and he'd been too bullheaded, too resentful to notice.

The obstacles and trauma she'd overcome humbled him, but there was more that he had to toss in her path. Was she strong enough to learn the truth about Eli? She loved his son. Their son. Eli adored her. The fallout from both of them learning the truth frightened him to his core.

"You expecting the fish to hop up here and grab the bait?"

Clay glanced at his dad as he took a seat in the other yard chair. "Just thinking."

"I know. This has been your thinking spot since you were a kid. Mine, too."

Clay waited for his dad to speak. He usually had something to discuss when he joined him at the pond. "What's on your mind?"

"Melody."

Clay groaned inwardly. "I know, Dad. I'm going to tell her. Soon. I promise."

"That's good to hear, but that's not what I want to talk about. The city council wants to meet with her about this Sergeant Croft matter. I'm afraid they're questioning her suitability for the project."

Clay sat up. "What? That's crazy. Why? She's worked hard putting this history together. Some days I don't think she ate or slept. She's determined to make it something the citizens can be proud of. She even suggested an idea for adding a blog to the town's website where people could upload their family histories and stories for everyone to read."

"That's a good idea. But right now, she has to answer some questions. The members want to make sure she's working to find the source of that damaging article."

Clay fumed, rubbing his chin. "This is ridiculous. If Eli hadn't shared that photo with his friend, there wouldn't be a problem. That whole article is just some sort of mistake."

"I think so, too. But if the council doesn't hear what they want, they could take action."

"What kind of action?"

The grim look on his father's face sent a jolt of alarm along Clay's nerves.

"You're not saying they'd fire her? Not at this late date—they can't. The book is almost finished. It's due next week."

Dave waved off his concern. "I know. Let's not get too wound up until we see what happens at the meeting. I've already explained the situation to Melody, and she promises to be prepared."

Clay's hands fisted on the arms of the chair. "Of course she will. She's the most conscientious person I know."

"Yet another of her sterling qualities."

Clay carried his anger and frustration to the airstrip a short while later. It took all his concentration to prepare the correct amount of product to spray the fields at Clover Hill Farms. Once in the air, his professionalism took over, but the moment he landed the Air Tractor, concern for Melody grabbed hold again.

He dreaded seeing her questioned by the council members, some of whom he'd had run-ins with himself. One in particular had a very narrow view of how things should work in Blessing. Tom Strickland would grill her ruthlessly on her work and her discovery of that old article. Clay wasn't about to let someone he loved face that ordeal alone. He'd be there beside her.

Wait. The truth of what he'd just thought hit him like a kick in the stomach. He loved Melody. He'd never stopped. Seeing her scars, learning of her life after she left—it had all shaken him deeply. He'd been wrong.

So very wrong. His actions back then and his decision to adopt the baby had been born of anger and hurt and a desire to lash out at her rejection.

Maybe he could make up for some of that by convincing the council that she should finish the book and that together they would uncover the reason behind that article.

Melody closed her laptop and spun in her desk chair to look at Eli. He was hard at work sorting through the last few photographs that needed to be returned to their owners. She had to smile at his diligence. He had a strong work ethic. But then she'd expect nothing less from Clay's son.

"Eli, I can't tell you how much I appreciate your help with this book project," she said. "Thanks to you, I was able to keep this project on track and get it turned in on time. You are a hard worker."

Eli shrugged self-consciously. "I guess. I liked helping you. But I really like taking pictures. I've asked my dad for a camera."

"Wonderful. I'm sure it would be more fun to take pictures of things you like instead of boring old photos and documents."

He grinned and nodded. "I like taking pictures of Barney and Lady."

Melody smiled. "They are pretty cute. I've taken a few pics myself." She glanced around her crowded office. "I need to get these books back to the library. Then I can start returning the rest to their owners. Would you like to come with me to the library? We can have ice cream when we're done. I haven't had a chance to visit the Ice Creamery yet."

"It's really good."

His enthusiastic endorsement made her smile. "Then let's get going."

Returning the books to the library took a little longer than expected. Deborah was busy with a reading group. When she finally joined them, she gave Melody the names of a couple of more residents who wanted to share their family history.

The ice-cream shop was nearly empty when they entered. Melody realized that it was late afternoon, so most people would be home preparing the evening meal. "I'm afraid I'm going to ruin your supper, Eli."

"That's okay. I'm always hungry."

Melody chuckled and placed their order. The clerk handed them their cones and a small paper bag, explaining that they were adding oatmeal cookies to the menu and were giving away free samples this week.

Melody and Eli took their cones outside to the table on the patio. It was a lovely afternoon.

"So is chocolate your favorite flavor?"

Eli nodded, taking another bite. "Do you like green ice cream?"

She held up her cone. "Mint chocolate chip. I have several favorites. This one is my pick today."

"Can we try the cookies?"

"Sure. Help yourself."

Eli slipped a cookie from the small bag and stared at it. After a minute, he began picking out the raisins. Melody grinned. "You don't like raisins?"

"Not in oatmeal cookies. I like them plain. And soft. Not crunchy."

She laughed and offered the boy her fist. "Me, too. I like to taste the oatmeal, not the fruit. I'll make you some soon. I have a great recipe. The cookies come out big and soft."

"Cool. Can I help bake them? Grandpa and I make cookies all the time."

"Of course." She pulled the other cookie from the bag and began picking out her own raisins, piling them on a napkin. "We'll have to tell the owner to make some cookies without raisins."

They shared a giggle.

The conversation centered on their book work and Barney's latest shenanigans. When they'd finished their treats, they started back to the car. Suddenly, Eli stopped and pressed his face to the glass of Kai's Kamera store.

"Wow. There're sure are a lot of cameras in there. How do you know which one to start with?"

Melody looked over his shoulder at the display in the window. It was daunting, trying to choose the right equipment. "Do you have a smartphone? You could start with that."

Eli shook his head. "I don't have one. Dad says I have to be thirteen before I can get one, which is like a million years from now."

"I suppose it is." She laughed. "Hopefully the years will pass quickly. How about I do a little research and I'll let you know what kind of camera you should start with so you can tell your dad."

Eli lowered his eyes before looking at her again. "Can you do that before July 12?"

"I think so. Why that date?"

"It's my birthday."

Melody couldn't breathe. July 12? Her child's birthday. Surely a coincidence. Lots of people were born on that date.

The rationalization didn't ease the tension in her chest.

The sensation was still with her when she met Sandy later in the evening at the dance studio where Sandy's daughter, Ava, took lessons.

They took a seat on a bench outside the studio to talk. Melody told her what had happened. Sandy stared at her for a moment, then shook her head.

"No. The birth date has to be a coincidence."

"That's what I keep telling myself, but I'm starting to find a lot of things don't add up. Clay says he fell in love with his wife quickly, and they had the baby right away. She died after Eli was born."

"So what about that bothers you?"

"We were in love. He would have to meet and fall for his wife immediately after we broke up. I can't see Clay falling for someone else so quickly."

"He fell for you that fast."

"I know, but if that's what happened, then…then he must not have loved me at all. He got over it really fast."

"Is that what bothers you? That he found someone else so quickly?"

Melody rubbed her cheek. "I don't know. Maybe. But what about Eli's birthday? He's ten. That makes the date and the year the same. Not close. The same! It doesn't make sense. Was he a preemie? He has to have been a preemie."

Sandy took her hand. "I think you're engaging in a little wishful thinking. You have a soft spot for Eli, and you wish he was yours."

She couldn't deny what her foster sister pointed out. "Maybe."

"There's no way Eli could be yours. You gave him up for adoption."

"I know. You're probably right. I do love Eli. He's such a sweet boy."

"He is. And he likes you, too."

"He said he wished I was his mom. It is weird sometimes. We have the craziest things in common. We both like peanut butter and banana sandwiches."

Sandy chuckled. "Hello, Elvis."

Melody thought back over some of her special moments with Eli. "I guess I was drawn to him right away. Sometimes I have this fierce affection for him. It scares me." Melody was silent for a few moments, then she stood. "I'd better go. I have that council meeting tomorrow night. I have to be prepared."

"I'll be praying for you."

The last fungicide application went smoothly, despite the threat of rain and his own preoccupation with the council meeting tonight. He'd told Melody he'd come by the cottage and drive her to city hall. There was no way he'd let her face that bunch alone. They'd try to railroad her, blaming her for the smear on Croft's reputation. But Melody would have all her ducks in a row, he was sure. She'd done everything possible to clear things up. Dragging her into the meeting was unnecessary and cruel.

His dad was sitting on the front porch when he arrived at the house, rocking away as if he hadn't a care in the world. Clay's nerves were frayed, and his protective instincts were running full force.

Clay took a seat in the other rocker. "Wish I could be that relaxed."

His dad grinned. "You will be as soon as I tell you my news."

"That the council has changed its mind about Melody?"

"Not quite, but I did get them to agree to discuss the matter without her being present."

"That's great. She's been through too much already. She's still fragile emotionally."

His father met his gaze. "What does that mean? Is something wrong with her?"

"Yes and no. You were right. She has been through a traumatic experience. You recognized it right away but I..." He chewed his lip. "Have you ever wondered why she always wears long sleeves, even when it's eighty degrees out?"

Dave shrugged. "I supposed she had a sensitivity to the sun or she burned easily."

Clay shook his head. "Do you remember that hotel bombing in Shanghai a few years ago? That was her office. She was one of only two survivors. Her arm was badly burned. She's been through a long and painful recuperation."

"Oh, that poor girl. I hate to hear that. I knew there was something wounded about her."

"I'm glad she doesn't have to face the council tonight."

"Well, she doesn't have to be present, but they still want to discuss the matter. A couple of them are very upset. They have questions."

"And I have the answers. Most of them anyway. As

the head of the book project, I can explain everything to them."

"Except the reason behind that article."

Clay shook his head. "I don't get it. Who cares? She's received confirmation from the military that our soldier earned his medal honestly. There's no question he was a hero. So why are they still poking around in this?"

"Well, they're still stuck on those conflicting dates on when his award was presented. And they're upset that Melody leaked that article. They suspect her motives."

"Melody didn't leak it! Eli did. And what motive would she have? She loves this town. She is heartbroken that she has stirred up a hornets' nest."

"I'm aware of that. I'm counting on you to stand up for her, be her defender."

"I will. I'm not going to let them do this to her."

Dave smiled. "Good man. That's what we do when we love someone."

Clay jerked his head toward his dad. "Love?"

"I've suspected for a while now that your feelings for Melody were returning."

He wanted to deny it, but he couldn't. He'd lied enough to his father as it was. So he shrugged. "Even if they are, it's an impossible situation. Once she finds out the truth, there will be no going back."

"Maybe, maybe not. You won't know until you confront the issue."

Clay refused to comment. His dad was a wise man, but he didn't understand the consequences of revealing the truth. Melody would surely hate him, and it could potentially destroy the relationship with his son.

Dad was right about one thing, though. He wouldn't

know for certain until he addressed the problem. He was right about another thing, too. Clay had fallen in love with Melody again despite his efforts not to.

"Have you told Melody she doesn't have to appear this evening?"

Dave smiled. "I thought you might like to deliver that good news."

Clay stood and started toward the cottage. At the edge of the pond, he stopped and looked back at the house. Dad had gone inside. Clay shifted his gaze to the cottage. Facing Melody right now wasn't a happy prospect. Not with his feelings so close to the surface. A phone call would be wiser. And safer.

Her cozy cottage had never felt so small. Since Dave and Clay had left for the council meeting in town, she'd tried sitting in her rocker on the porch, working in her office, walking around the pond and even doing laundry, but nothing could keep her mind off the outcome of that meeting. Would they fire her and let someone else complete the book? That seemed overly harsh, but she'd angered a lot of people with that article. If only she'd kept it to herself. But she'd been so intent on making the Blessing history the best it could be, she hadn't wanted to leave anything out. And she'd believed that article was significant.

A light breeze, heavy with the scent of gardenias, lifted her hair as she stepped back out onto the porch. Darkness had settled over the property. Moonlight spilled across the pond and sparkled off the ripples. It was a beautiful sight, but she had no one to share it with. Eli wasn't even home to keep her company this evening. He was spending the night with a friend. It was probably just as well. She'd grown too attached to the boy. It would be difficult to leave him behind when she moved away from Blessing.

She touched her fingertips to her lips. It would be hard to leave Clay, as well. They'd grown closer this last week. His tenderness about her scars and her ordeal had toppled the final barrier around her heart.

Sandy had been right when she'd asked if Clay was the reason she'd never loved again. She'd given her heart to Clay and nothing that had happened since had changed that. The obstacles between them now were external and unchangeable. No matter how much she loved him or how much she regretted her decision about their child, she couldn't go back and fix it.

Her only wish now was that Clay and Eli would have a happy life and maybe she could keep in touch with them going forward. Why were humans so short-sighted? Why did they think they could control destiny and that what they did when they were young wouldn't have any effect on their lives down the years?

Headlights flashed as a car turned into the drive. Melody held her breath. What had they decided? She closed her eyes and prayed softly. "Lord, whatever the outcome, give me the strength and courage to go forward with my life. Thank you for bringing me here to Blessing and reuniting me with Clay, even though I don't deserve it."

A shadow appeared along the drive. Melody recognized Clay's physique. The broad shoulders, the long easy stride, the way his shoulders dipped slightly as he walked. She stood and clutched the porch rail, every nerve in her body tensed for bad news.

He topped the steps and came to her side. He was smiling.

"Well?"

"You are still the book lady."

"Oh, thank You, Lord." Her hand went to her throat and she exhaled a heartfelt breath. She touched Clay's arm. "What happened? What did they say?"

"Between Dad and me, we reminded them that the book was almost done and due at the printer's in a few days if it's going to be published for the bicentennial. We also pointed out that the article was leaked to the newspaper and the editor had failed to fact-check before printing." He smiled. "And we presented your letter from military records confirming that our Sergeant Croft did indeed accomplish the mission and was given the award."

"So everything is good?"

He shrugged. "All except Tom Strickland. He's convinced that you have some nefarious reason for exposing that article and he wants it settled. Yesterday."

"He's the only one still upset?"

"And he's likely to be that way from now on." Clay shrugged. "He gets upset about a lot of things that no one else even worries about."

"Oh, Clay, I'm so relieved. I don't know what I would have done if they'd made me leave."

"I wouldn't have let that happen. Not until you were done. You've worked too hard."

"Thanks. I appreciate that."

Clay looked into her eyes, and her heart skipped a beat. She knew that look. She'd seen it many times. That glint of attraction, the invisible cord that vibrated between them when they were close. Instinctively she placed her hand on his chest, above his heart. It was beating rapidly, in time with hers. His hand came to rest on her jaw, gently tilting her face upward.

"I'm glad you're not leaving."

"Me, too. But I will be going home eventually."

He trailed his finger along her jaw. "I know. But we need to talk before you do."

"What about?"

"About the past. Us. Mistakes."

"Oh."

"I know." He stepped back, his eyes still locked with hers. "But let's get through this book project first. Then we'll sort it all out."

"All right."

"I'd better go. I have to figure a big job for tomorrow."

"And I need to finalize the book."

At the bottom of the porch steps, Clay turned and looked back at her. "You're beautiful in the moonlight."

She caught her breath, watching him until the shadows swallowed up his tall form. Did he mean that? Did he still care? She knew the attraction was still there. It pulsed between them each time they were close. Sadly, she knew that attraction wasn't enough.

Melody rose the next morning more rested than she'd been in a long while. Knowing she could finish the book had allowed her to rest worry free. But today she had to tackle the details. With a few days' work, she could present the finished manuscript to Clay, knowing she'd done everything possible to make the Blessing history project one the town would treasure.

Of course, that left the matter of the rogue article. Even when her job was complete, she promised herself she'd keep digging until she found the truth. Gathering up a small stack of books, Melody headed from the cottage and across the yard to the Reynolds house. She had some books to return to the family library. Clay had a proud heritage. He had the family tree she'd always fantasized about. She knew nothing about her own history. Her mother never talked about her family and her father was only a name in her memory.

Did Clay understand what a blessing he'd been given? Did he appreciate his lineage? What would it be like to look back and see a long line of grandparents and relatives and trace their accomplishments?

She entered the Reynolds home from the French doors that led directly to the library. It was a small room in area but large in ambiance. She always felt as if she'd stepped into an old English estate. Dave had told her the library wasn't used much and they'd thought about turning the room into something more useful. The thought made her sad.

She placed the books on the desk, then picked up the first one and found its place on the shelf. She had just slipped the last book into its spot when she noticed the photo albums on the next shelf.

She'd seen them before, but now she was consumed with curiosity. What had the Reynolds men looked like when they were younger? She slipped out one small album with Eli's name on it. She had no doubt that he'd been a beautiful little boy, the spitting image of his father.

She opened the cover, expecting to see a newborn picture of Eli, but he looked to be a few months old. He was a sweet baby. She smiled, gently touching her fingertips to the picture. Her gaze lowered to the notation below.

Eli Clayton Reynolds. July 12. 6 lbs., 4 oz. 1:34 a.m.

The album fell from her nerveless fingers, landing on the desk with a thud.

Her baby had been born at the same time. Exactly the same time. Surely it was a coincidence. It had to be. She was reading more into the date and time than what was real. Her affection for Eli was clouding her mind. How many times had she secretly wished he was her son. How many times had she thought about the little child she'd given up and what a horrible mistake it had been.

"He was a beautiful baby, don't you think?"

Melody spun around at the sound of Dave's voice. Her cheeks flamed. "I'm sorry, I didn't mean to snoop."

Dave waved off her concern. "Nonsense. You're practically family now." He came to her side and turned a few pages in the baby book. "That little boy saved my sanity."

"What do you mean?"

"My wife, Clayton's mother, had lost her battle with cancer shortly before Clay brought Eli home. I wasn't in a good place, but having that baby here, watching him grow, took my mind off everything else. He brought me joy every day. He taught me how to laugh again and to find hope in every day." He gently touched a photo of Eli. "He was the biggest blessing of my life. I couldn't have made it through without him."

Melody's heart melted. "Thank you for telling me that. I can understand why y'all are so close."

Dave chuckled. "Listen to you, using *y'all* properly. You are a certified Southerner now." He handed her the baby book. "You're right. We are close. But there's always room for one more. Here—enjoy. If you have any questions, just ask."

Melody pondered his words as she studied the baby album, memorizing every photo and every entry. How she would have loved to watch Eli grow.

How she would have loved to see her own child grow.

But she'd forfeited that opportunity for an empty dream.

Chapter Eleven

Melody's cell phone broke her concentration on the files she was searching. Absently, she picked it up without looking at the screen. "Hello."

"Miss Williams. My name is Lana Talbot. My grandmother saw an issue of your local paper and the article about Sergeant Croft. I have some papers that I think you should see. I'd like to meet with you. I'm coming to Blessing this afternoon."

Anticipation made her smile. "Yes, Mrs. Talbot. I'm anxious to see what you've found. Shall we say around three o'clock? My office is in the courthouse annex."

"Thank you. I'll see you then."

Melody placed her hands on her cheeks, bubbling with excitement. The information this woman had might answer all the questions about Sergeant Croft. She'd like nothing more than to settle this question before she left Blessing.

She cleared a space on her desk and removed the small file box from the only other chair in the room. She wanted her office to look neat and professional when Mrs. Talbot arrived. Casting her gaze upward, she whispered a heartfelt prayer of gratitude, only to have reality slither into her thoughts. It might not be good news at all. It could be nothing but an insignificant antidote to his life and not an explanation of the article at all. Or it could be worse. Either way, she had decided to put an end to the issue. She had to accept that she might never learn the truth.

Hopefully, when the book was published and in the hands of the citizens, the whole thing would fade away and be nothing more than an odd bit of Blessing history. But she couldn't keep her hopes from soaring at the prospect of a solution to the whole mess.

She'd checked the clock and glanced out her small annex office window a half a dozen times before a woman appeared in her doorway.

"Miss Williams. I'm Lana Talbot."

Melody wasted no time in coming to the point. "I hope you have some answers for me. That article has upset the whole town."

"No doubt." She handed Melody a thick journal and a small stack of letters. "I think these will answer a lot of your questions. It's a love story. An unusual one at that."

Melody studied the old journal, its cover cracked and discolored with age. A rubber band held it closed. "I hadn't anticipated a romantic explanation. How did you come across this?"

"As I mentioned, my grandmother saw the article in the paper and called me. She said she knew about that article and why it was never printed. She gave me these documents and asked me to contact you and give you these. She wanted you to know the truth. Your soldier, Sergeant Croft, was a relative of ours."

Melody touched the journal. Finally, an answer lay

within these old pages. "I don't know what to say. I'd hoped for some explanation, but I never dreamed I'd meet someone related to our soldier." Melody leaned her arms on the desk. "Can you tell me why the article was written?"

Mrs. Talbot nodded. "It's all in the journal. The romantic part is at the end. The journal belonged to Alice Garland. The letters are from a suitor, Nathan Merritt."

"How does he fit into the story?"

"He's behind the whole thing." She crossed her legs. "I'll give you the short version, and you can read the rest for yourself."

Melody poured them both a glass of tea then settled in to hear the tale.

"My great-great-grandmother was Alice Garland. Her father owned the Blessing bank. She was very pretty and had two suiters, Linwood Croft and Nathan Merritt, whose family owned the newspaper. When war broke out in 1914, Linwood joined up and went off to fight. Nathan was classified 4-F and had to stay home. He continued to court Alice, but her heart belonged to Linwood.

"When the war was over, Linwood came home a hero but a changed man. However, Alice loved him, and they became engaged. Nathan was heartbroken. He'd watched out for Alice while Croft was away, but she remained true to her love.

"Nathan noticed Linwood was different. He had drastic mood swings and bursts of anger. Nathan began to worry about Alice's safety, but she was blind to his faults. She only saw him as a noble hero. Nathan wrote the article out of spite and printed up a phony front page, hoping to open Alice's eyes and stop the wedding. But it didn't work. Alice was furious and refused to believe ill of her fiancé.

"Alice and Linwood married, but their happiness was short-lived. Linwood was gassed during the war and he's dying. Alice is expecting. Nathan decides to settle for being Alice's friend, and he continues to watch over her."

Mrs. Talbot pointed to the journal. "I must admit I feel sorry for the man. He loved my great-great-grandmother deeply and had to stand by and watch her love another, though his tactics were totally misguided."

Melody was captivated by the story. "What happened to Nathan?"

Mrs. Talbot chuckled softly. "That's the best part. Alice and Nathan eventually fell in love. They got married, and he raised Linwood's son as his own. According to the journal, they had a very happy life together."

Melody grinned. "Incredible. And the false article?"

"Forgotten, I'm sure. It's amazing it survived at all. I imagine Nathan tucked it away and forgot all about it. No one ever saw it but the two of them. Nathan was the one who proposed the statue in Sergeant Croft's honor. He wanted to give Alice some comfort."

Melody grinned. "This is a fabulous story. Thank your grandmother for this." She touched the journal. "I'll get these back to you as soon as possible."

Mrs. Talbot stood. "No need. She asked that you donate them to the local historical society or perhaps the library when you're finished. I hope I've helped clear up any questions."

"You have. The people of Blessing will be relieved to know that there are no black marks on their hero's reputation." She shook the woman's hand. "And person-

ally, I'm relieved to be absolved of any ulterior motives
toward defaming their beloved citizen."

Melody called Clay the moment Mrs. Talbot left but
it went to voice mail. She couldn't wait to show him the
journal and letters. And she couldn't wait to devour
every word herself.

Clay parked his car near the garage, taking a moment to gather his thoughts. He had bad news to deliver to his father, and he dreaded the conversation. He
wanted to stop at the cottage and talk to Melody first.
She had a way of looking at things that always eased
his concerns. But he didn't.

He hurried toward the back door instead, avoiding
the puddles along the way. Putting off this discussion
wouldn't help. He found his father in the living room,
reading. Dad glanced up and smiled. It faded immediately. Clay could never disguise his worry. He took a
seat, leaning forward, his elbows on his knees.

Dad closed his book and frowned. "What's wrong?"

There was no good place to start. "Jared received an
offer from Delta today. He's seriously considering it.
I offered him a raise, but we can't compete with their
number."

Dave tugged on his ear. "I was afraid of this. I suppose I could start flying again to help out."

Clay shook his head. "That's not a good idea, given
your medical history. It's too risky."

"We can hire another pilot."

"Dad, I'm afraid that's not possible. I think we need
to look at more drastic measures. I can fly the jobs now
since demand is light, but the second planting season is
here, I won't be able to meet the orders."

"What are you suggesting? Selling the company? Has Delta approached you?"

"No. Not yet. If this rain would let up, we might be able to keep going. I can't remember a spring this wet. And we're not the only ones affected. The farmers can't get crops in the ground if the rain doesn't stop."

Dave stood and placed a reassuring hand on Clay's shoulder. "We'll be all right. We can sell the planes if it comes to that."

"I can try to fly for someone else."

Dave shook his head. "I don't like that idea. We're not going to close up yet. We'll think of something."

Clay started to argue, then decided to let the thing go for now. Nothing would change in the short term, and he might be able to convince Jared to stay on.

His phone rang, and Clay pulled his cell from his pocket. Melody. He answered reluctantly, his thoughts on his father and the business.

"Clay, I have wonderful news. I've solved the puzzle about Sergeant Croft. A Mrs. Talbot contacted me, and it seems her great-great-grandmother had two beaus, and one of them was related to the editor of the paper. He tried to discredit Croft in her eyes by creating a false article."

"That sounds cruel."

"Strange and misguided for sure, but it was all motivated by love. I'm going to write an article for the *Banner* explaining everything."

"That's a good idea. It'll smooth all those ruffled feathers. Melody, I'm glad you have that worked out. I know the people of Blessing will be relieved. Thanks for letting me know. I'm sorry, but I have to go. I'll talk to you later."

He hung up knowing he'd been rude, but he had to deal with company problems right now. Dad went to his small office and started making phone calls. Clay had no idea what good that would do. He'd already looked into the options he could think of, but if it made Dad feel like he was helping, he wasn't going to get in the way.

He glanced out the front window and saw Eli and Lady fishing at the pond. They must have gone outside the moment the rain had stopped. He needed some clarity. Maybe a trip to the bridge would help. He had no answers to any of his problems at the moment.

The cottage didn't feel as cozy this evening. Melody had been feeling restless since she'd talked to Clay on the phone. He'd been pleased that the rumors about Sergeant Croft were finally cleared up, but he'd been distracted. His mind was obviously on something else, his company perhaps. He hadn't said much, but she knew things weren't going well. Dave had made a few remarks, too. She'd added the Dusty Birds company to her prayer list.

Still, Clay's attitude bothered her. She'd expected him to be overjoyed, maybe even suggest a celebration. Instead he'd cut the call short without even an explanation.

She needed to talk to him. She had questions about the baby book and that coincidence of the dates. Plus, she needed to clear her conscience. Clay needed to know the whole truth. With her job on the book complete, she'd be leaving town soon. She would hand him the final manuscript in the morning. She was out of time.

But maybe she needed an objective opinion. Her feelings for Clay were clouding her judgment, and she had no idea how to untangle things. It was time to talk to her sister.

Sandy arrived at the cottage within minutes. "What's wrong? You sounded so strange on the phone."

Melody sighed and clasped her hands. "Do you want the good news first or the bad?"

"Good, always." Sandy sat down at the kitchen table and plucked a fresh cookie from the plate.

"The mystery of the rogue article on our soldier has been solved. You'll love the explanation. It's very romantic."

"That's good to hear. And the bad?"

"I've discovered another detail about Eli that troubles me." Sandy waited patiently. "I was returning some books to their library when I saw his baby book. It had his time of birth. 1:34 am." She watched for her sister's reaction.

Sandy's brows rose and her eyes widened. "Oh. That's...odd."

Melody chewed her lip. "So you think it's more than coincidence?"

"I... It's curious to say the least. What are you thinking?"

"I'm not sure. So many things have puzzled me since I came here. Clay's resentment I understood, but his determination to keep me away from Eli made no sense. I asked him once about his deceased wife, and he brushed me off. What if he was trying to keep me away because he didn't want me to find out Eli was mine?"

Sandy frowned and held up her hands. "Whoa. You are running off the rails here, sis."

"I know, but...what about the other things? Like the way I feel when I'm around Eli? I was drawn to him from the first moment. And we like the same kind of unusual foods, like chocolate popcorn and oatmeal cookies without raisins."

Sandy frowned. "That's hardly proof he's your child."

Melody stood and paced the small kitchen. Her nerves were frayed yet her instincts told her she was onto something. "What about the timeline? Clay would had to have met someone, fallen in love, gotten married then pregnant, then the wife had to get sick and die, all within a few months. And that's not possible."

"Maybe it was somebody he knew before you, an old girlfriend."

"I suppose. But if that's true, then Clay never loved me at all. Not if he could go back to her so quickly after we broke up."

"I know the date and time are curious, but I'm sure there are other people who have the same stats. Besides, how would it even be possible? You gave the baby to a family. Right?"

Melody clenched her teeth. "Did I? I only have the lawyer's word for that. They'd insisted they remain anonymous. They were celebrities or something."

"Still, given the way you and Clay parted, do you really think he'd adopt the baby? You said you didn't leave a note. He had no idea where you went."

"I know." She rubbed her temples. "But it was his baby and, knowing who he is… Once he knew about it, I can't imagine him not trying. Only I didn't give him a chance." She plopped onto a kitchen chair. "It's probably my mind playing tricks, indulging in wishful thinking. I wish I could go back and do it all over."

"There's one way to find out," Sandy said dryly. "Ask him."

"I plan to. As soon as possible."

Sandy rose and came to her side, giving her a sisterly hug. "I suggest you do it before you leave Blessing. You and Clay both deserve to know the truth. Let me know when you do, and I'll be there to pick up the pieces."

Melody smiled. "You always are."

Melody paced her small living room, her gaze darting to the front window anxiously. She'd asked Clay to come over. She was going to confront him and ask him outright if Eli was her son. She had to know one way or the other. Logically, there was no way it could be true. Still, she couldn't shake certain details about the adoption and the curious requests made by the adopting family. They'd wanted no contact with her, no questions asked. The lawyer had told her the family was well-known and didn't want publicity. And in exchange for that utmost privacy, they covered her hospital expenses.

She looked out the window again in time to see Clay step onto his front porch. Her heart seized up. She couldn't rest until she confronted him, but if she was wrong, he'd never forgive her and their budding friendship would be over. Her heart would be broken again.

But if she was right, wouldn't the outcome be the same? He wouldn't let her into Eli's life. And what about Dave? Would revealing the truth hurt him, as well? He'd told her about his closeness with Eli; the family bond was deep and secure. Would learning the truth ruin that?

The sound of footsteps on the porch stilled her breath. She sent up a quick prayer for strength and opened the door. He was so handsome. Tall, lean and with those clear blue eyes, was it any wonder she'd fallen for him?

"Melody? What's wrong? You sounded upset." He

entered, then turned to face her, his puzzled expression drawing his brows together.

She clasped her hands together tightly to still their shaking. "I need to ask you a question, and I need you to give me an honest answer."

"All right."

Her courage flagged, heat rushed through her body, her forehead broke out in a sweat and her palms became clammy. Her heart pounded fiercely. She couldn't do this. Whatever the answer, her heart would be shattered.

"Melody. Are you all right?"

She wanted to run, avoid everything. But deep down, she knew she couldn't hide from this any longer. It was too important. She took a deep breath.

"Clay, is Eli my son?"

The blood drained from his face. His shoulders braced and he held her gaze a moment before turning his back.

"Why would you ask me that?"

"Because his birthday is the same as my...our baby. You won't talk about his mother, there are no pictures and Eli knows nothing about her. He doesn't like raisins in his oatmeal cookies." She knew she sounded like an idiot, but she didn't care. She had to know.

"You're not making any sense."

"I know that. None of it makes sense, but I have a feeling... I mean, I think... I—"

Clay moved to stare out the window. He was silent a long time. She heard the long, shaky breath he drew. And then he answered.

"Yes. He's our son."

The words fell into her heart in icy fragments. She struggled to wrap her mind around his words. Her knees weakened and she sank onto the sofa. She didn't know whether to laugh or cry, hug Clay in joy or hit him in fury.

She placed her cool hands on her flaming cheeks, struggling to arrange her thoughts into some sort of order. "How? Why?"

Clay looked as shell-shocked as she felt. Not since the bombing had her mind been so disjointed and confused. She stared at Clay as he started to speak.

"I was angry when you disappeared without a word. I couldn't believe you'd tell me you were pregnant and then walk out. I didn't know what you were planning to do."

"Nothing horrible. I would never—"

Clay held up his hand. "I know. But it took me months to track you down. I had to hire a private detective. Then when I found you, I learned you were giving the baby—my baby—up for adoption. So I contacted an attorney. He took care of everything."

Melody sorted through what he'd told her. "You adopted your own child? Why didn't you just claim him as yours?"

Clay sighed and dragged a thumbnail across his eyebrow. "I don't know. Because I would've had to involve you. I didn't think you'd cooperate."

"Or were you too angry?"

"I was. I won't deny it. I was furious. So, yeah. I was determined to keep you out of it. You didn't want our child, but I did."

His hard tone pierced her heart. "I wanted him, Clay. I didn't think I did when I left you but…" Her voice trailed off. She took a breath. "But I had no choice. I had no way to take care of him. I wasn't *able* to be a mother. I didn't know what else to do."

"Giving him to strangers was the only option?"

"Yes." She stared at her hands. "Or that's what I thought at the time. But I've regretted it every day since. I've never stopped thinking about him, wondering where he was, worrying whether he was happy and loved, being cared for. Every birthday, I've cried myself to sleep, wondering what he looked like, how he was doing."

She wiped tears from her cheeks. "I didn't think of it before I did it, but after he was gone…I worried every day that he might have ended up like me—living in foster care with strangers instead of with people who loved him. And because of the agreement, *our* agreement, I couldn't find him."

She stopped and looked at Clay. "Thank you for loving him and taking care of him. I'm so grateful that you did."

"He's my son."

The overwhelming relief of knowing her child had been loved and cared for gave way to the anger of being lied to and kept away from her son. She stood.

"And mine. You decided without telling me that you should take our child and raise him. Then, when I came here, you did everything in your power to keep me from finding out. And you've lied to Eli, his whole life. That's unforgivable."

Clay ran a hand through his hair. "I know. At first, I was angry and hurt and it all made sense. It wasn't until I brought Eli home to Blessing that I began to realize what a tangled mess I was making. By that time, I was in too deep. There was no way out."

"You found me once. Why didn't you try again?"

"I assumed you were living your big life. You'd made your choice. I made mine." He met her gaze. "If I'd found you, would you have wanted to be Eli's mother?"

She didn't have an answer for that. Not one that he would understand.

"You had no right to keep me in the dark. Not to mention what you've done to Eli. He thinks his mother is dead! How could you?"

Clay whirled around. "How could I tell him his mother didn't want him? How could I explain to him that his mother gave him up to strangers?"

Melody sank into a chair. "I guess there's no easy solution is there? We were both wrong."

"Yeah."

"But I want him to know the truth, Clay, all of it. It's not fair to any of us this way. We can't continue with the lies."

"You sound like my dad."

"You *told* him?"

"I really intended to tell you, Melody, but every time I tried I—"

"Chickened out?"

"Something like that. Then you and Eli grew closer, and he started asking questions. I couldn't see a good outcome, no matter what I did."

Melody stood. "When can we tell him?"

Clay set his jaw. "I don't know. I'll have to find the right time."

"No. *We'll* tell him. I've learned the hard way, the right time never comes. Postponing only leads to more trouble."

"We have to take Eli's feelings into consideration."

He set his hands on his hips. "We can't just drop it on him—his mother isn't dead, and I've been lying to him his whole life? I can't do that."

Melody wanted to be angry, to lash out and defend her position, but he had a point. This was Eli's life they were talking about.

How would their son react to Clay's deceit? And how would he feel when he learned she was his mom and had given him up? What kind of defense could she offer for her decision? A selfish one. She'd chosen her career over her child.

Clay had his own reasons. He'd let his broken heart and his anger create a wall of lies around his son, a wall that had grown taller with each year. Now they both had to find a way to dismantle it and still protect Eli.

"So what do we do?"

"I don't know. I know what we need to do. I just don't know how to go about it. Any suggestions?"

She shook her head. "No matter how I envision it, the outcome isn't good. I don't want Eli to hate either of us. Maybe your father could help. Be a mediator of sorts."

"Maybe. I'll talk to him. In the meantime?"

"Leave things alone. But this can't go on much longer. I've found my son, and I want him to know who I am, that I love him."

Clay nodded. "So do I."

Melody stood stiffly as Clay went to the door. He looked back, his blue eyes troubled.

"I'm sorry, Melody. Really. I handled everything badly. It was vindictive and that's not me. You know that."

"I know. But I think there's enough blame for both of us."

They'd both made poor choices. If she'd met up with him the next day… Even if she'd still turned down his proposal, they could have worked out a solution. But she'd been too selfish, too determined to make something out of her life. She sighed. "We were so young, Clay."

"But old enough to know better." He opened the door. "Eli is coming across the lawn. Do you want me to give him a reason to stay away today?"

Melody's thoughts and emotions swirled. Having Eli here would be so wonderful now, knowing he was her son. But how could she be close to him and not tell him who she was?

"Yes. I'm not sure I can be around him right now. I need time to think."

"Okay. Will you be all right?"

She nodded. "I'll be fine. But we have to end this soon. Very soon."

"I know."

Clay left, and she watched him high-five Eli as they met. Then he turned their son toward the house, laying an arm across his shoulders. She turned away from the poignant sight.

Was telling Eli the right thing? Would it shatter the family he'd known all his life? She was his mother. She had rights… Or did she? Hadn't she relinquished them when she'd signed the papers?

Chapter Twelve

Melody barely remembered making her way out of town toward the Blessing Bridge, but every time she'd looked out the window, she'd seen the Reynolds home, and the merry-go-round of emotions had started spinning again. She'd needed to escape, so here she was.

A red SUV was parked in the Blessing Bridge lot when Melody pulled in. She waited, hoping the visitor would leave soon. She needed alone time at the site. After a few minutes, a young woman emerged, entered her car and drove away.

Melody walked slowly toward the entrance, her legs moving as if made of lead. Her heart pounded and her thoughts spun around in circles like a windmill in a strong breeze.

Slowly, the woodland smells penetrated her troubled mind. A faint scent of honeysuckle hung in the air and random azalea bushes added splashes of color along the path. Acorns crackled beneath her feet. The light breeze stirring the leaves played with her hair and calmed her nerves.

By the time she stopped at the top of the arched

bridge, her head had cleared. She gazed at the still water in the large pond. Sunlight sparkled on the ripples. There really was a serenity about this place. She'd doubted the stories she'd heard and had taken the whole Blessing Bridge legend with a grain of salt. But getting her prayers answered here wasn't as important as absorbing the quiet comfort the place offered.

In this peaceful place, it was easy to shove aside the day's concerns and turn your mind toward spending quiet time with the Lord.

Be still and know that I am God.

The verse popped into her mind and made her smile. She knew He was God, but that didn't tell her what she was supposed to do now that she'd found her son. Was showing her what she'd given up part of God's plan? Was He reminding her of what a huge mistake she'd made?

She reached out and plucked a lavender blossom from the vine winding around the railing. The wisteria was delicate and fragile, like her thoughts. What was she supposed to learn from this?

Through every trial she'd faced, the Lord had shown her new knowledge—of herself, of life and mostly of His gracious nature. Should she take comfort from knowing Eli was safe, happy and loved? That had been her prayer for the last ten years, and He had answered it. She could live on knowing her child was in the arms of a loving family. His father's family. *She could.*

No, she couldn't. Now that she knew the truth, how was she supposed to walk away and pretend she hadn't spent weeks working with him, being part of his life? How could she be close to him now and resist the need to hold him close, to love him the way a mother would?

How could she leave Blessing now? And would Clay agree to let her visit or at least keep in touch with Eli?

Tossing the flower into the pond, she wiped the tears from her eyes. Finding her son should have made her deliriously happy, but it hadn't. It had only raised a new pile of questions and obstacles.

Maybe Clay was right. Telling Eli was a mistake. How would he react?

Melody covered her face with her hands. *Lord, I don't have an answer. I don't know which way to go. Show me the way. Show me what's best for Eli.*

Clay looked up as his son hurried into the room later that day and handed him the newspaper.

"Did you see the cool article Miss Melody wrote about our soldier? It takes up the whole front page! Guess this means everybody won't be mad at her any more."

Clay scanned the article, secretly surprised that Aaron had agreed to print the entire thing. Melody must have sweet-talked him into it. "I hope so. She wasn't to blame."

"I know. It made her sad that nobody liked her."

"It did? How do you know that?"

Eli shrugged. "I could see it in her eyes. They'd get sad-looking whenever people said bad stuff to her."

Clay squeezed his son's arm. "You like her a lot, don't you?"

"Yes, sir. I liked helping her. I wish she could stay here."

Clay wished that, too. He wanted her to stay. That couldn't happen until they resolved this mess, but he had no idea how to do that. Both options were painful and would hurt Eli. On the other hand, ignoring the problem was unfair to everyone.

"Dad, are we grilling burgers tonight? Can Miss Melody come, too? It'll feel like a real family then."

"Sure," Clay responded. Eli pumped a fist in the air and turned to leave, but Clay called him back. "What do you mean, Eli, a real family?"

The boy shrugged. "You know. Like a mom and a dad and a grandpa."

A lump clogged Clay's throat. "The three of us are a family, aren't we?"

"Yes, but most of my friends have a mom. I don't. I wish I did."

Clay's stomach clenched. "You never said you wanted a mom."

Eli lowered his head. "I didn't want to make you mad. You don't like it when I ask about my mom."

A wave of shame surged through Clay's system, highlighting all the errors he'd made in the last ten years. He pulled his son to him and held him close.

"I'm sorry, son. I didn't mean to make you afraid to talk to me. I promise we'll have a long talk very soon about…your mother. There are a lot of things I need to explain to you."

"Okay. Will you call her and ask her to supper?"

What? Oh, Melody. "Sure."

Clay rubbed his forehead, trying to ease the raw ache inside his skull. He'd never asked himself what his son was missing in not having a mother. He'd focused all his energy on being the best father he could, believing that he and his dad were family enough. He realized now that Eli would always be missing that one piece every child needed. And he had denied him that piece his whole life.

Clay pulled out his cell phone and called Melody. It went to voice mail. Relief settled over his mind. It was just as well. He had some soul-searching to do. Something he should have done a long time ago.

Melody's car was in the parking lot at the Blessing Bridge when Clay pulled in. He started to pull out again, then realized he was following his old pattern of avoiding difficult situations. He parked and started down the shaded path to the open sunny area where the bridge stood. He saw her standing at the railing, looking straight ahead, the breeze flirting with her auburn hair.

He stopped at the foot of the bridge, suddenly as tense and anxious as a schoolboy.

Father, what do I say? How do I make amends? I've hurt her so badly. It hit him then that the majority of his prayers were about the easy things in life. He prayed for health and safety, for Eli and his dad, and for his business to succeed.

He hadn't realized until now that he even avoided the hard stuff with God. He'd never asked for help in letting go of his resentment or to forgive Melody. He'd never asked to be shown his own failings.

He stared at Melody, still standing quietly at the top of the bridge. He loved her. Always had. He loved his son. He wanted them both in his life. *Lord, help me face the truth. Help me do what's best for Melody.*

He stepped up onto the bridge. "Melody." She turned and he heard her catch her breath.

"How did you know I was here?"

He moved closer. Her beauty in the fading light took his breath away. "I didn't. I came for some quiet time."

She smiled. "Me, too. I'll go and leave you alone."

He caught her hand as she started past and held it, warm and soft, in his. "Don't go. Maybe this is where we need to be right now to work things out. We weren't doing well on our own. We need someone wiser, don't you think?"

She smiled and pulled her hair back with both hands. "I know I do. I want to do what's best for Eli, no matter what that means."

"I want to do what's best for all of us. I don't want to you hurt again. You're too important to me."

She reached out and laid her hand on his arm. "You've always been important to me, Clay. I just got lost along the way. I'm so sorry. Can you ever forgive me?"

He took her hand. "I'm the one who should be asking for forgiveness. I created an impossible situation for all of us. You know that Eli loves you, right? He wants you to stay in Blessing."

She nodded. "He told me once that he wished I was his mother. It was so sweet, and I was so touched. Now that I really am his mother, I don't know what to do. I don't want him to hate me when he learns the truth."

The tears in her eyes broke Clay's heart. He pulled her close and rested his cheek against her silky hair.

"He won't. We'll explain it to him. We'll tell him how much we loved each other but that we made mistakes. He'll understand."

Melody turned her face up to him, and his love for her returned full force. She whispered his name, and he lowered his head, placing a light kiss on her lips. The sense of belonging, that belief that they were meant to be together, was as strong as ever. He didn't know how it would work out, but for the first time since she'd walked out of his life, he knew they would be all right.

A notification from his cell phone broke the spell, and he glanced at the text. "It's Dad. He needs to see me." He took Melody's hand, and they walked off the bridge toward the parking lot. He didn't want the moment to end. Now at least, he had hope that somehow it would all work out for all of them.

He helped Melody into her car, then bent down and touched her cheek. "We'll talk soon."

She nodded with a smile. His heart swelled with love stronger and more powerful than he'd ever known.

It didn't hit him until he was halfway home that he hadn't actually prayed at the bridge. Or maybe he had.

The Dusty Birds office was tiny; it barely had room for a desk and the necessary files. Clay entered and saw his dad hunched over the computer. When Dave glanced over his shoulder at him, Clay was stunned to see how old he looked. He didn't want to think of his dad getting older, but he couldn't ignore it any longer. His hair was grayer, the lines in his face were deeper and the worry in his blue eyes was alarming.

"What's up, Dad? You don't usually spend time here anymore."

"I know. I just wanted to look things over, see if I could find some way to ease the strain on the business. Where've you been?"

Clay rested a hand on his dad shoulder. "I was at the Blessing Bridge."

"Oh? In need of a little spiritual consultation?"

"In a way. Dad, we might not have to worry about the future of Dusty Birds anymore. I heard some interesting information this morning. I ran into Sheriff Hughes and he told me the owners of Delta Agricultural Applications have been arrested for fraud and a few other felonies. The company has been shut down."

Dave slapped the top of the desk with his palm. "I told you I had a bad feeling about that bunch. They rose too fast, gobbling up smaller companies, hiring away the best people." He glanced at the screen. "So does this mean we'll be all right?"

"It means we keep Jared on the payroll. Our biggest enemy now is the weather. But I think we can work around that. It might not be a banner year profit-wise, but we won't go under."

Maybe revealing the truth to Eli wouldn't sink the family either. They all wanted the same thing. The truth. It might sting for a while, but surely they'd find a way to work it out.

Melody entered the Reynolds house through the back door the next day and hurried into the kitchen. Dave was at the sink rinsing out a coffee mug.

"How is he?" Her heart pounded as she searched his face for some clue about Eli. Dave had called her to let her know Eli wasn't feeling well and had asked her to come sit with him while he picked up some cold medicine.

"He's resting, but I've made an appointment with his physician for later this afternoon. I don't like the looks of him."

"Is that all it is, a cold?"

"Probably, but I think it might be settling in his chest. He had a bad case of bronchitis when he was seven, so we keep an eye on him any time he gets a cold. You sure you don't mind staying with him? I won't be gone long."

"I'm happy to do it. I love that boy."

Dave's gaze slid away from hers, and she caught a glimpse of something odd. Was he keeping something from her? Was Eli sicker than he was letting on? "Can I peek in on him?"

"Sure. He might be waking up. He's been resting awhile."

Melody peeked into Eli's room, expecting to see him snuggled under the covers. Instead she found him sitting up in bed and gasping for air. Ice shot through her veins. She recognized that sound. Wheezing. *Asthma.*

"Dave!"

He was at her side in an instant. "Call the ambulance!"

Melody pulled out her phone, her heart pounding, her mind a dark cloud. Nothing could happen to Eli. She'd just learned he was her son. She couldn't lose him now. She backed against the wall, paralyzed, watching as Dave spoke softly to Eli, urging him to be calm.

She barely breathed herself until the paramedics arrived. She was struggling to make sense of what was happening. Dave walked behind the gurney as they moved Eli to the ambulance. He told her to meet them at the hospital.

All she could do was beg the Lord to spare her child.

She moved by habit and instinct, barely aware of her movements. Keys. Steering wheel. Roads. Parking.

The emergency room was crowded, every space occupied. She searched for Dave.

Where was he? Where was Eli? What was happening? She hurried to the desk.

"I'm looking for Eli Reynolds. He was brought in by ambulance."

"Are you family?"

Her heart chilled. "No, but—"

"Then I'm sorry."

A scream rose in her throat. She wanted to demand to see him. She was his mother. Why hadn't she told them that? She loved him. She paced the waiting area, peering down hallways, hoping to catch a glimpse of Dave. She finally saw him seated on a bench, his head bowed, clearly worried. Her heart chilled.

"Dave?"

He looked up, the lines in his face more pronounced, the pain in his eyes scratching at her hope. He took her hand and tugged her down beside him.

"He's breathing normally again."

"Oh, thank God! Do they know what caused it?"

"Not yet. I don't understand. He's not allergic to anything that I know of."

"Does Clay know?"

Dave nodded. "He's on his way. He should be here shortly. He was top cropping a field over in Alabama."

"He must be beside himself."

The doctor came out and took Dave aside. Melody held her breath, waiting and praying for Eli until the doctor walked away. She searched Dave's face for a hint of reassurance. He took her hand.

"They're going to run some tests, but the doctor thinks it might be an asthma attack."

"I didn't know he had asthma."

Dave rubbed his forehead. "He doesn't. I just don't understand."

Melody squeezed his hand. "We'll know more after the tests."

Time passed in a haze of gnawing fear and fervent prayer. She longed to visit the bridge for some much-needed quiet time, but she couldn't leave the hospital until she knew Eli was going to be all right.

In her mind, she kept replaying the moment she'd realized Eli was struggling to breathe. The moment she'd been wrenched back to another time, a time when she was eight. When that sense of helplessness had first paralyzed her.

She glanced again at the waiting room entrance, hoping to see Clay. Her heart ached for him. He must be terrified. Eli was his world.

The next time she looked up, Dave was coming toward her. She jumped up, heart thudding like thunder in her chest. He gave her a hug. "He's going to be fine. The doctor thinks it's late-onset asthma."

"Is that common?"

"No, but it's not unheard of. If that's the case, then we'll be looking at making some changes in his life. In all our lives."

"Dad." Clay hurried toward them. "What happened? How is he? Can I see him?"

The fear exuding from Clay tore at her heart. She didn't have to imagine what he was feeling. She felt it, too. Only for him, it must be ten times worse.

Dave gripped Clay's arm in a comforting manner, attempting to calm his fears. "He's fine now."

"What happened?"

"We're not sure. He wasn't feeling well. I thought it was a cold. Melody came by to stay with him while

I went to the store, but when she entered his room, he was struggling to breathe. That's when we called 911."

"I want to see him."

Dave indicated the small alcove. "He's asleep."

Clay returned a few moments later and sat down, scraping his fingertips across his scalp. "I can't lose him."

Dave rested an arm across his son's shoulders. "We won't. The doctor said he'll be fine. They are going to keep him overnight for observation, though."

Neither of them noticed her in their tight moment of familial connection. Melody suddenly felt out of place. As much as she loved Eli, she wasn't part of this family. They needed to deal with this themselves. Quietly she stood up and moved away. She pushed aside the disappointment cutting through her veins. Foolishly, she'd wanted them to ask her to stay, to include her in the wait.

She stopped at the nurses' station and asked directions to the hospital chapel. She found it tucked away in a quiet section on the second floor. Taking a seat in the back, she let the sweet peace of the room calm her raw nerves. Her gaze focused on the burnished cross on the wall behind the altar as she searched for words to pray for her son. She couldn't find any. Thankfully, she knew words weren't really necessary for prayer. Her groaning would be understood.

Clay sat by his son's bedside, sending up prayers of gratitude without ceasing. He'd sent his dad off to get something to eat. Eli was sleeping, and the doctors had assured him he'd be fine when he woke up, though probably scared. The doctor had given him a preliminary rundown of the situation. He had a lot to learn about caring for an asthmatic child.

Unfortunately, no one had answers as to why this had happened. The best they could tell him was that, sometimes, it just happens. The serious bronchitis he'd had a few years ago might have been an indicator of what was to come, but there was no way to say for certain.

They'd told him how close Eli had been to dying when the paramedics arrived. He couldn't even allow himself to think about that.

Clay sensed his dad entering the room. "He's still asleep."

His dad squeezed his shoulder. "I'm so sorry. I should have paid closer attention. I thought it was just a cold."

"Don't, Dad. It wasn't your fault. No one could have seen this coming."

"I suppose not. All I know is that Melody and I were in a full panic. I'm surprised she could even think straight to call 911."

Clay frowned. "Melody. She was there?"

"Yes, of course. She came by to sit with Eli while I went to get cold medicine. She followed me here and waited until she knew he was going to be all right. She was distraught to say the least. She was here when you got here."

Clay ran a hand down the back of his neck. "She was? All I saw was you. Is she in the waiting room?"

"Not now. Maybe she went home."

Clay shook his head. "She wouldn't leave without seeing Eli." He reached over and held his son's hand, silently urging him to wake up.

"Clay, I think this might be a good time to tell Melody the truth."

At least this was one thing Clay could settle. "I already told her. She'd figured it out when she saw Eli's baby book."

His dad mouthed a silent *oh*.

Before either of them could say anything more, Eli squeezed Clay's hand. Relief surged through him as he looked into his boy's wide eyes.

"Hey, buddy. Welcome back."

"What happened?"

Clay brushed the hair off Eli's forehead. "They think you had an asthma attack."

Eli frowned. "I couldn't breathe. I was scared."

"I know. But it'll be all right now. We'll just have to pay attention to what you do and maybe change a few things. Don't worry. We'll figure out what set you off, then we'll take care of it."

Eli smiled at Dave. "Hey, Grandpa."

"Hey, kiddo. You gave us quite a scare."

"Where's Miss Melody?"

Clay exchanged a look with his father. "I'm not sure. Would you like to see her?"

Eli nodded.

Dave patted Eli's leg. "I'll see if I can find her."

Clay released his son's hand and stood. "No, Dad. I'll find her. I want to talk to the doctor, too."

In the corridor, Clay let the emotion take over. Tears stung his eyes as his chest contracted painfully. He leaned against the wall. He could have lost everything this afternoon. His whole world could have ended. But God in His grace had allowed Eli to survive. "Thank You, Lord," he whispered.

Pushing away from the wall, he went in search of

the chapel. He needed some alone time before he talked to Melody.

Clay located the chapel easily and slipped inside. Someone was already there. He started to leave when he realized it was Melody. He weighed his options. Should he find another place to be alone or join her?

Before he could decide, she turned and saw him, only to quickly look away and bow her head. There was no way he could leave now.

He took a seat beside her, waiting for her to speak. He stole a glance and realized how upset she was. She loved Eli. There could be no doubt about that.

He reached over and took her hand. "You all right?"

"I will be. I'm just so grateful that he's all right. I didn't know what to do. He was fighting to breathe, and I felt so helpless, just like when—" She stopped.

"When what?"

"Nothing. How are you?"

"Grateful. Thankful. Blessed."

Melody nodded. "I'm so glad. I couldn't stand it if anything had happened to Eli."

Clay pulled her close. Offering comfort and needing some himself.

"Do the doctors know what caused it?"

"Right now, they're saying it's late-onset asthma. I don't understand it, though, because there's no history of asthma in our family. Apparently, it can be hereditary."

"Hereditary?"

Clay's phone buzzed. He pulled it out and read the text. "I have to go. The doctor wants to meet with me. Do you want to come? Eli's awake and he's asking to see you."

Melody shook her head. "I need a little more time here. I'll find you."

Clay studied her expression. There was a strange look in her eyes he couldn't define. "All right." He squeezed her hand and was rewarded with a small smile. "We'll be waiting in Eli's room. They've put him in 312."

"Clay, tell Eli I love him."

He smiled. "I think he knows that, but I'll tell him."

He stepped into the corridor, then glanced back at the chapel door, uneasy. There was a strange note of finality in her tone, almost as if she were saying goodbye.

He shook off the notion. His emotions were too jumbled to think clearly.

Chapter Thirteen

The moment Clay left, Melody bent over in pain. Her heart burned; her mind was wrenched in two. It was her fault! Eli had inherited his asthma from her. Her mistakes kept compounding. Now her son would suffer the rest of his life from an illness he'd gotten from her. The mother who was supposed to protect him had condemned him to a life of restrictions. How could she tell Eli the truth now? She'd given him another reason to resent her and hate her.

Her chest constricted, making it hard to breathe herself. There was only one thing to do. It was time to leave Blessing. It was best for everyone. Clay would hate her, too, when he realized that Eli's asthma was her fault. She had to do what was best for Eli, even if that meant giving him up. Again.

Time to go to the only place she'd ever belonged.

A few days later, safe in her foster mother's home, Melody curled up in the floral club chair near the living room window and looked out on the spring landscape at Mama Kay's. As lovely as it was, her heart longed for Blessing. She missed Barney, too. She could use some of his furry comfort right now. She'd put him in the garage with Lady when she'd left, and she'd left the jump drive with the completed Blessing history book on the desk in the Reynoldses' library.

She'd severed every tie.

A shaft of pain lanced through her veins as she thought of Clay and Eli. Eli, her son. Her prayers had been answered far beyond her deepest dreams. He'd been raised in a loving home, and he was happy and safe. It was more than she'd ever expected. God had made it all work for good, just as He promised.

The only thing missing was her. That lovely family picture would never include her.

"I thought I'd find you here." Mama Kay settled in her rocker, peering at her from over her glasses. "You always curled up here when you were troubled."

"Did I?"

Mama Kay nodded. "I knew you had something scary on your mind when I found you here. Sandy preferred the window seat in her room."

"I never realized we were so predictable."

"Most people are." Mama Kay faced her. "Talk to me. I can't help if you don't share."

Melody brushed her hair from her forehead. "We talked it all out last night."

"No, you told me what happened. You didn't tell me why you ran away again."

"I didn't run away. I did what was best for Clay and Eli."

"Did you? Or did you do what was easiest for you?"

She bristled at the suggestion. "Of course not. I want Eli to have the close relationship he's always had with his father. He can't have that if we tell him the truth. He'll be angry at both of us."

"You don't know that. You said you and the boy had grown close. How do you know he wouldn't be delighted to learn you are his mother?"

"Not when he realizes I gave him up."

Mama Kay shrugged. "Maybe at first. But I imagine he'd come around. Love is a great motivator. Of course, you won't know that until you stop running and turn around and face this."

"I am not running away." Melody set her jaw. Her foster mother was usually so wise and comforting. Not confrontational.

Mama Kay scooted forward in her rocker. Then she reached out and touched Melody's scarred arm. "You've been running since the moment you came to me, Melly. You ran away to college in Georgia, you ran away from Clay when you got pregnant. You even chose a career path that would keep you running from place to place so you wouldn't have to stop and look at yourself too closely. Frankly, I think you've been running since your little brother, Ronnie, died."

Melody's heart skipped a beat. She'd never talked about that. To anyone. "How do you know about him?"

"I like to know about all my kids, especially the ones I get close to like you and Sandy. Ronnie wasn't your fault. You were eight years old."

Melody chewed her lip, as the old memory pulled her down. "I should have been able to do something to help him. But Mom wasn't home and there was no medicine and when he couldn't breathe, I didn't know what to do."

Mama Kay moved and sat beside her. "Of course you didn't, but you're all grown up now. It's time to look at what happened and accept you're not to blame. You don't have to run anymore."

Melody shook her head. "No. Eli has asthma because of me. He inherited it *from me*." Her throat closed up. "What if he has an attack, and I can't help him?"

"Melody. You're an adult. What would you do in that situation?"

"I don't know."

"Think. What would you do?"

She tried to think logically. Step by step. "I'd make sure he always had medicine on hand. I'd learn what to look for, to recognize when an attack might happen. I'd call the doctor or an ambulance if necessary. I'd make sure he had—" She stopped as realization settled in.

Mama Kay patted her arm. "See? You're not a child anymore. You're not your mother. You would take care of Eli, make sure he had his medication."

The clouds surrounding the death of her brother began to clear. For the first time she looked at the situation through the eyes of a grown-up. Not the child she'd been.

Mama Kay sat back, a satisfied smile on her face. "Now, what are you going to do about Clay? Don't you think it's time you stopped running away from him, too?"

Melody shook her head. How could he love someone like her? "No. Things between us are too complicated."

"No, they're not. You're just running away again. You've faced the truth about Ronnie and about Eli. Don't you think you should find out what the situation is with Clay?"

"I don't know."

Mama Kay stood. "Well, I do. He'll be here in an

hour. Go get dressed and start clearing away the cob-
webs in your brain. Decide how you really feel and
what you really want. No more running or denial. It is
time for you to turn around and deal with life, sweetie.
Trust me. It'll work out for the best."

Melody fought the knot in her chest as she got ready
to see Clay again. She changed clothes three times, finally settling on a dark gray skirt, a white blouse and
her favorite denim jacket that always made her feel
confident. It wasn't working very well today, however.

The doorbell rang as she ran a brush through her
hair. Her heart stopped beating. What would she say to
him? How could she explain and make him understand?

Mama Kay's assessment of her behavior had stung,
but the more she thought about it, the more she realized it was true. She'd spent her whole life running
away. Did she have the courage now to stop and walk
toward the future?

She closed her eyes and listened as her foster mother
greeted Clay. She couldn't make out what they were
saying, but she knew Mama Kay would be warm and
gracious.

Time to face the music. Taking a deep breath, she
opened the door and stepped into the hallway, walking
toward the only man she'd ever loved.

Clay stood anxiously in the cozy living room, waiting for Melody to appear. He'd been stunned when
Mama Kay Davis had called and told him Melody was
with her. When he'd realized Melody had left, he'd been
furious, then hurt, then puzzled. He'd been torn between
finding her again and leaving her alone. Eli had been

upset. Before he could decide what to do, however, he'd gotten the phone call.

What if Melody didn't want to see him? Mama Kay had told him Melody was heartbroken, that she loved him and Eli, but had some misguided notion that they'd be better off without her in their lives. He was here to convince her otherwise.

"Hello, Clay."

He turned and saw her, and his heart leaped into his throat. She'd been gone only a few days, but somehow she was more beautiful than he remembered. The light blue denim jacket highlighted the pink in her cheeks.

"Hi."

An awkward silence hung between them. She pressed her lips together, then gestured toward the sofa. "Have a seat."

He sat, unable to take his eyes off her. "You look good."

"You, too."

He opened his mouth to speak but she beat him to it. "How's Eli?"

"He's fine. Back to normal. We're still adjusting to the situation. It'll take a while to work out all the do's and don'ts. He misses you, too. He wants to know when you're coming home. He was very upset you left without saying goodbye."

Melody wrapped her arms around her waist. "What did you say?"

Clay grinned. "I told him the truth. I didn't know why you'd gone." He kept his distance, not trusting his emotions if he got too close. "Why *did* you leave again?"

She turned away. "I'm sorry I left the way I did, but I

told you, I'm not cut out to be a mother. You have good paternal instincts."

"Why would you say that? You're great with Eli. He loves you. I've seen the bond between you."

Melody shook her head. "No. You don't understand. It's my fault he got sick."

He had no idea what she was talking about. "That's ridiculous. No one's to blame for that."

"I am. You said the asthma was hereditary. He inherited it from me." She crossed her arms and looked at the floor. "I had a little brother. His name was Ronnie. He had asthma. He died when he was six."

Clay's heart wrenched. "I didn't know. How old were you at the time?"

"Eight."

Clay took a step toward her. "That must have been—"

She faced him, her eyes filled with pain. "It was my fault he died."

She couldn't be serious. "You were a child."

Melody turned away, wringing her hands. "He had an attack, and he couldn't breathe. I couldn't help him." Her voice broke.

Clay wanted to go to her, but he sensed she was too fragile to accept his comfort right now. "Where was your mother?"

Melody wiped her eyes. "Um. Mom left us alone. She did that a lot. She'd been gone two days when Ronnie had the attack. He didn't have any medicine, our phone didn't work and I couldn't do anything to save him."

Clay's chest constricted. "I'm so sorry. That's a horrible thing for a child to go through."

She shrugged. "That's when I went into foster care.

When I was fourteen, I came to live with Mama Kay, and my whole life changed."

His heart hurt for her, but he had to ask. "I still don't understand why you left, Melody."

She turned and faced him. "I'm the reason Eli has asthma now. He inherited it from me. I couldn't save my brother from his asthma attack—what if I can't save Eli? It's too big a risk. He's better off without me. All he needs is you."

Clay went to her, taking her shoulders in his hands. "That is not true," he protested. "It's just something that happened. No one's to blame. For all you know, he could have inherited his asthma from a distant relative of mine."

He pulled her around to face him. "Melody, you're not making sense. Eli won't be left alone, and he'll have everything he needs. I'm new to this asthma thing, too. We can learn together how to care for Eli."

Melody shook her head. "No. It's too big a risk. He's my son. I'd do anything for him."

"Even give him up? Again?"

She raised her chin. "Yes. I'll do what's best for him."

Clay grinned and touched her cheek. "What if the best thing for him is to have both his parents taking care of him, and becoming a complete family, the way they should have been?"

Tears filled her eyes. "No. When he finds out who I am, he'll hate me."

Clay pulled her a little closer. He understood that fear. He'd lived with it for ten years. The chance that Eli could hate him had locked him into a position of secrecy and denial. But he had good news.

"I know how you feel, Melly. I lived with that fear a

long time. I thought if I told Eli about you, about how I lied to him about his mother, he'd hate me." He looked into her eyes. "But I've already told Eli everything."

She gasped, her eyes wide. "You should have left it alone."

"I told Eli the truth after you left. He was confused about why you gave him up for adoption, but I explained how young we were and how life gets complicated when you grow up. He was a little angry at first, but Dad and I talked to him and helped him understand. As much as a ten-year-old can anyway. Basically, he's thrilled that you're his real mother. He's liked you from the first moment. Oh, and he made me promise to tell you he would take good care of Barney."

He took her hand. "If he's angry with anyone, it's me. I didn't have a very convincing reason for keeping the truth from him."

"What did you tell him?"

"The truth. That I was angry and hurt and wanted to punish you by raising him and not telling you. I told him how wrong I was." Clay laughed and shook his head. "He told me that I should remember Pastor Miller's sermon on forgiveness. He's an amazing kid. He took what I thought was so complicated and reduced it down to one word."

"I'm glad for you. But will he forgive me?"

"He already has. He wants you to come back. So does Dad."

She pressed her lips together. "You're just saying that. I wouldn't be able to face him."

Clay stiffened. He'd expected her to be relieved and happy. "What's this really about, Melody? What are you afraid of?"

She met his gaze for a moment, then looked away and moved off. "Mama Kay says I have a habit of running away from anything hard or difficult, which is strange because I always thought I was running toward life. But she's right. I don't know how to stand and face life."

"I don't believe that. You told me you're a different person, that the explosion gave you a new perspective on life."

"It did, but you and Eli need someone strong and solid. I left you the first time because I didn't know how to stand and work things out. I ran from Shanghai because I didn't know how to restore my dream, and I'm running now because I don't know how to be a wife and mother."

"I could say the same thing, Melody. I don't know how to be a husband. I've never been one before. But I do love you. Eli loves you. My dad adores you. Don't you think, with all that love and support, we could work this through together?"

Her brown eyes were filled with doubt. "Why would you do that?"

"I told you—I love you. I never stopped loving you."

"After what I did?"

"Is it any worse than what I did? I was so angry. So hurt."

She touched his cheek, her gaze caressing his face. "I'm sorry. I never meant to hurt you. I loved you. I still do."

"Then don't we owe it to ourselves and to Eli to be a family? It's what he wants. It's what I want."

Her eyes welled up. "I do, too, but I don't want to fail."

"You won't. You're stronger—*we're* stronger—than

you think. Neither of us is alone in this. We have each other and as long as we keep the Lord in our plans, we'll be all right."

"He's given me so much. Now He's given me a second chance to be a wife and mother."

Clay held her closer. "And he's given you a job if you want it. That idea you had about a Blessing Blog, Dad took it to the council, and they approved it. They want you to take charge. It's only a part-time position, but who knows where it could lead?"

He slipped his arms around her waist. "Melody, you know I love you. I fell for you the moment we met. Marry me and be my wife and Eli's mom, the way you were meant to be. We belong together, the three of us."

He drew apart, gently taking her scarred arm in his hand. "We've both gained scars over the years, Melody. Yours are on the outside. Mine are on the inside. It's time to let them heal and move on. The past is behind us."

"I want to, Clay, but I'm afraid."

"I am, too. But we can face the fears and the future together. I'm sorry I adopted Eli without telling you. I see now how wrong and hurtful that was. I never took your position into consideration. Or Eli's. We should have made that decision together."

"I'm sorry for running away and not giving you my answer."

"Will you marry me and help me raise our son?"

Her gaze locked with his. He saw the love shining in her golden-brown eyes, and his heartbeat quickened.

"Yes," she breathed. "Oh, yes."

He pulled her into his arms and kissed her with the love he'd held in his heart for ten years. She kissed him back, chasing away any lingering doubt about her love for him.

When they moved apart, he slipped two plane tickets from his pocket. "We can catch the flight home if you hurry and pack."

Melody laughed, releasing a sweet warmth through his body.

She slipped her arms around his neck. "I don't need to take much. Everything I need is back in Blessing."

Epilogue

Melody stole a glance at Clay in the driver's seat. His strong profile sent a ripple of appreciation along her nerves. They were coming home. They'd spent the flight back to Mississippi talking about a million things. There'd been a decade to catch up on. She smiled as they passed the Dusty Birds sign and drove past her sweet cottage. But when he stopped the car near the main house, her anxiety rose.

Coming face-to-face with Eli, now that he knew the truth, had her heart in her throat. Clay had assured her Eli was excited that she was his mom. What if he was just saying that to make her feel better?

She exited the car as Eli burst through the front door. Clay came around and took her hand. He must have sensed her tension. She bit her lip as her son approached, a big smile on his face.

He stopped a few feet away. "Hi. I didn't think you'd ever get here."

She stared at him, letting her gaze cherish every detail of his face. "The plane was a little late."

Eli shifted his weight. "I'm glad you're my mom."

Melody caught her breath. "I'm glad, too."

"So, can I call you Mom now? Is that okay?"

Her vision blurred with tears, she could only nod.

Eli stared at the ground a moment. "Could I give you a hug? Would that be okay?"

Choked with emotion, she opened her arms. Eli rushed forward and held her tight. Clay slipped his arm around her shoulders. She sent up silent prayers of thanksgiving. This morning, she couldn't imagine a happy solution to her life, but the Lord in his gracious nature had made a way.

A sharp bark and little paws on her calves broke the poignant moment. Barney refused to be ignored.

Eli chuckled. "He's missed you. He kept going over to the cottage. I tried to tell him you weren't there, but he kept running over anyway."

Melody scooped up the furry dog and cuddled him. "I missed him, too."

"There's been a lot of missing going on around here."

Melody smiled at the familiar voice. "Hello, Dave."

"Welcome home, Miss Melody." He wrapped her in a warm hug. "I told Clay if he came home from Iowa without you, I'd disown him."

Melody leaned into Clay, who had his arm around her waist now, making her feel protected and loved. "I'm glad. He can be slow at times."

Dave snickered. "Tell me about it. I've been hounding him all along to clear the air between you."

"You mean, you knew the whole time?"

"From a few days after you arrived."

That explained so much. She wasn't sure if she should be upset about that or not, but right now she was too happy to think of anything else. She had her son and the man she loved in her life. And maybe a father, too.

Dave stepped behind Eli and grasped his shoulders. "Why don't you two take a few minutes to relax at the pond," he suggested. "Eli and I have a few things to finish up in the house. We'll call you when we want you."

"What kind of things?" Clay asked.

Dave raised his chin. "Never mind. You'll find out soon enough." He waved them away, then turned and walked with Eli back into the house.

"I guess we've been sent to our rooms." Clay took her hand and started toward the two Adirondack chairs under the live oak at the far end of the pond. "I wonder what those two have cooked up."

Melody held his hand, enjoying the contact. For so long she'd felt adrift and lacking roots. Now she had Clay and Eli and Dave and a proud family history.

They sat down, still holding hands. "Do you think you can be happy here, Melody? It can't compete with the noble plans you once had."

Melody smiled. "I used to think being an international correspondent was my 'noble purpose,' like in the Bible verse."

"I don't understand."

"You know, the one that says God is the potter and he has the right to make some pots for noble purpose and some for common use. I've come to see I had it backward. An ornate pot is placed on a pedestal to be admired but rarely used. A common pot is used every day to service a family, to provide sustenance, and then it's cleaned and used again. It's worn out in servicing others."

She looked at Clay. "That's the noble purpose. To serve. I don't want to be a beautiful pot that's left to be admired." She squeezed her hand. "What more noble purpose can there be than being a wife and a mother? Whatever else I do takes a back seat to that."

He pulled her to her feet and kissed her, a kiss filled with the promise of a lifetime. Finally, he leaned back and smiled down at her.

"I have something for you. I've had it for a very long time. I didn't think I'd ever be able to give it to you, but now…" He slipped his hand into his pocket and pulled out a ring.

She gasped. "Clay!"

He took her hand and slipped the sparkling diamond on her finger. It fit perfectly. "I'd been planning to give you this that night. But then everything changed."

She stared at the ring, twinkling in the sunlight. "You've had it all this time?"

He nodded. "I think the Lord wanted me to hold it until he could work things out. He knew we were meant to be together, but we just weren't ready yet."

She slipped her arms around his neck. "I'm glad he had a plan because mine wasn't working out."

"His plans usually do work out better than our own, don't you think?"

He started to kiss her again, but Dave called from the porch.

"Come on, you two. Plenty of time for that lovey-dovey stuff later. We have a celebration in here."

Hand in hand, they started back across the lawn to the house. They had much to celebrate today. And the promise of many celebrations to come.

God was good.

All the time.

* * * * *

If you loved this tale of sweet romance,
pick up these other books
from author Lorraine Beatty:

Her Fresh-Start Family
Their Family Legacy
Their Family Blessing
The Orphans' Blessing

Available now from Love Inspired!

Find more great reads at www.LoveInspired.com

Dear Reader,

I hope you enjoyed your visit to Blessing, Mississippi. Both Clay and Melody made decisions during an emotional crisis that only led to more problems later on.

Melody made her own choices that created a burden of regret and guilt.

Both wanted to protect those they loved—Clay wanted to protect his son, Melody wanted to protect Clay.

The only way out of the tangled mess they had created—even though they both had good intentions—was to seek forgiveness and reveal the truth, even if that meant losing one another.

Forgiveness isn't easy for anyone. We all carry the perception that if we forgive someone who has wronged us, then we're saying, "It's okay. You're excused." The truth is forgiveness is for our benefit. To lift the heavy burden of never-ending anger and desire for revenge.

I hope you enjoyed this second visit to Blessing, Mississippi. I love to hear from readers, so feel free to contact me at my website, lorrainebeatty.com, or like my author page on Facebook, Lorraine Beatty Author, or follow me @LorraineBeatty on Twitter.

Lorraine

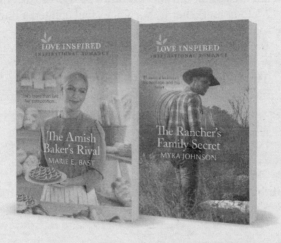

HIDING HER AMISH SECRET
The Amish of New Hope • by Carrie Lighte
Arleta Bontrager's convinced no Amish man will marry her after she got a tattoo while on *rumspringa*, so she needs money to get it removed. But taking a job caring for Noah Lehman's sick grandmother means risking losing her heart to a man who has his own secrets. Can they trust each other with the truth?

TO PROTECT HIS CHILDREN
Sundown Valley • by Linda Goodnight
Struggling to find a nanny for his triplets, rancher Wade Trudeau advertises for a housekeeper instead. So when former teacher Kyra Mason applies, looking for a place without children to recover after a tragedy, she's shocked to meet his toddlers. Might this reluctant nanny and heartbroken cowboy find healing together?

A PLAN FOR HER FUTURE
The Calhoun Cowboys • by Lois Richer
Raising his orphaned granddaughter alone seems impossible to Jack Prinz, but he has the perfect solution—a marriage of convenience with his childhood friend. But even as Grace Partridge falls for little Lizzie, convincing her to marry without love might not be so easy...

THE TEXAN'S TRUTH
Cowboys of Diamondback Ranch • by Jolene Navarro
Returning to his family ranch, Bridges Espinoza's surprised to find his cousin's widow—the woman he once secretly loved—there as well. But even more stunning is the boy who arrives claiming to be his son. While the child brings Bridges and Lilianna together, the truth about his parentage could tear them apart...

THE SHERIFF'S PROMISE
Thunder Ridge • by Renee Ryan
After Sheriff Wyatt Holcomb and veterinarian Remy Evans clash over her new petting zoo—and her runaway alpaca!—the two strike a bargain. She'll watch the nephew in his care for the summer if he'll push along the permit process. But keeping things strictly professional is harder than either of them expected.

SEEKING SANCTUARY
Widow's Peak Creek • by Susanne Dietze
When pregnant single mom Paige Latham arrives in Kellan Lambert's bookstore needing a temporary job, he wouldn't dare turn away the sister of his old military buddy. But as they grow closer working together, can they say goodbye before her baby arrives, as planned?

Get 4 FREE REWARDS!

We'll send you 2 FREE Books plus 2 FREE Mystery Gifts.

Love Inspired books feature uplifting stories where faith helps guide you through life's challenges and discover the promise of a new beginning.

FREE Value Over $20

YES! Please send me 2 FREE Love Inspired Romance novels and my 2 FREE mystery gifts (gifts are worth about $10 retail). After receiving them, if I don't wish to receive any more books, I can return the shipping statement marked "cancel." If I don't cancel, I will receive 6 brand-new novels every month and be billed just $5.24 each for the regular-print edition or $5.99 each for the larger-print edition in the U.S., or $5.74 each for the regular-print edition or $6.24 each for the larger-print edition in Canada. That's a savings of at least 13% off the cover price. It's quite a bargain! Shipping and handling is just 50¢ per book in the U.S. and $1.25 per book in Canada.* I understand that accepting the 2 free books and gifts places me under no obligation to buy anything. I can always return a shipment and cancel at any time. The free books and gifts are mine to keep no matter what I decide.

Choose one: ☐ **Love Inspired Romance Regular-Print** (105/305 IDN GNWC) ☐ **Love Inspired Romance Larger-Print** (122/322 IDN GNWC)

Name (please print)

Address   Apt. #

City   State/Province   Zip/Postal Code

Email: Please check this box ☐ if you would like to receive newsletters and promotional emails from Harlequin Enterprises ULC and its affiliates. You can unsubscribe anytime.

> Mail to the **Harlequin Reader Service:**
> **IN U.S.A.:** P.O. Box 1341, Buffalo, NY 14240-8531
> **IN CANADA:** P.O. Box 603, Fort Erie, Ontario L2A 5X3

Want to try 2 free books from another series! Call 1-800-873-8635 or visit www.ReaderService.com.

Arleta had tossed and turned all night ruminating over Sovilla's
and Noah's remarks. And in the wee hours of the morning, she'd
come to the decision that—as disappointing as it would be—if
they wanted her to leave, she'd make her departure as easy and
amicable for them as she could.

"Your *groossmammi* is tiring of me—that's why she wanted
me to go to the frolic," she said to Noah. "She said she wanted to
be alone. And if I'm not at the *haus*, I can't be of any help to her,
which means you're wasting your money paying me. Besides, her
health is improving now and you probably don't need someone
here full-time."

"Whoa!" Noah commanded the horse to stop on the shoulder
of the road. He pushed his hat back and peered intently at Arleta.
"I'm sorry that what I said last night didn't reflect the depth of my
appreciation for all that you've done. But I consider your presence
in our home to be a gift from *Gott*. It's invaluable. Please don't
leave because of something *dumm* I said that I didn't mean. I was
overly tired and irritated at—at one of my coworkers and… Well,
there's no excuse. Please just forgive me—and don't leave."

Hearing Noah's compliment made Arleta feel as if she'd just
swallowed a cupful of sunshine; it filled her with warmth from

her cheeks to her toes. But as much as she treasured his words, she doubted Sovilla felt the same way. "I've enjoyed being at your *haus*, too. But your *groossmammi*—"

"She said something she didn't mean, too. Or she didn't mean it the way you took it. If I know my *groossmammi* as well as I think I do, she felt like you should go out and socialize once in a while instead of staying with her all the time. But she knew you'd resist it if she said that, so she turned the tables and claimed she wanted the *haus* to herself for a while."

That thought had occurred to Arleta, too. "*Jah*, perhaps."

"I'm sure of it. I can talk to her about it when—"

"*Neh*, please don't. I don't want to turn a molehill into a mountain." Arleta realized she should have spoken with Noah before jumping to the conclusion that neither he nor Sovilla wanted her to stay. But she'd been so homesick yesterday, and she'd felt even more alone after she'd listened to the other women implying how disgraceful it was for a young woman to work out. Hannah's lukewarm invitation to the frolic contributed to her loneliness, too. So by the time Sovilla and Noah made their remarks, Arleta already felt as if no one truly wanted her around and she jumped to the conclusion they would have preferred to employ someone else. She felt too silly to explain all of that to Noah now, so she simply said, "I shouldn't have been so sensitive."

"*Neh*. My *groossmammi* and I shouldn't have been so insensitive." Noah's chocolate-colored eyes conveyed the sincerity of his words. "It can't be easy trying to please both of us at the same time."

Arleta laughed. Since she couldn't deny it, she said, "It might not always be easy, but it's always interesting."

"Interesting enough to stay for the rest of the summer?"

Don't miss
Hiding Her Amish Secret *by Carrie Lighte,*
available May 2021 wherever
Love Inspired books and ebooks are sold.

LoveInspired.com

LOVE INSPIRED

INSPIRATIONAL ROMANCE

UPLIFTING STORIES OF FAITH, FORGIVENESS AND HOPE.

Join our social communities to connect with other readers who share your love!

Sign up for the Love Inspired newsletter at **LoveInspired.com** to be the first to find out about upcoming titles, special promotions and exclusive content.
